I0770658

THE SOUL SHIELD

BOOK TWO OF
THE TENDRILS OF LIGHT SERIES

VICTORIA M. SORENSON

Library of Congress Catalog-in-Publication Data has been submitted for application.

Editor: Alexis Askew

@alexisaskew_writes

Cover Art and Marketing Design: Rena Violet, with Covers by Violet

@violet.book.design

Interior Design and Formatting: Victoria M. Sorenson (Yours Truly)

ISBN:

Paperback 979-8-9916087-3-2

Hardcover 979-8-9916087-5-6

Ebook 979-8-9916087-4-9

This book contains content with themes of grief, loss, and overcoming traumas.

I have intertwined relatable thoughts and feelings with my characters' progression on their road to healing. I want my readers to know that their mental health is essential, regardless of age or gender.

I hope and pray that my stories help validate your feelings because even the not-so-fun emotions are crucial for moving forward during difficult times.

I see you. I hear you. You are loved.

To include a wide variety of readers, I have decided to make my books **plot-driven, with no explicit language, and with closed-door romance.**

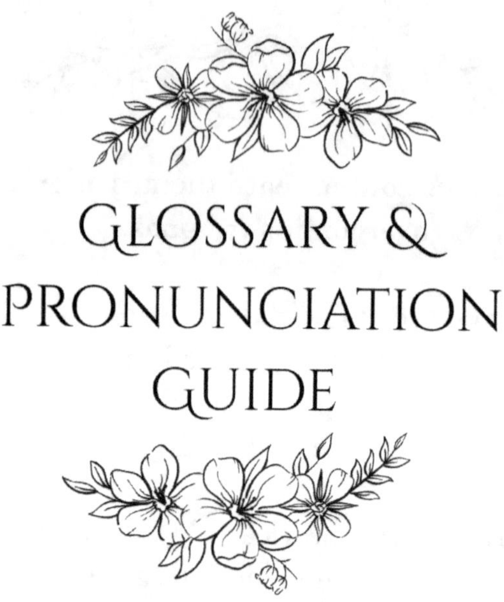

GLOSSARY & PRONUNCIATION GUIDE

Time Explained:

A complete moon cycle: One month has passed.

A single moon: One day has passed.

Thirteen Moon cycles: One year has passed.

Creator   **kree-ay-tor**

The consciousness born into existence out of darkness is responsible for the gift of the *Marked Ones*. It assisted in the making of the *Videira*, the sacred vine. All species and cultures recognize it as the higher entity.

Ligação Mágica   lee-ga-sow ma-jee-kuh

The green-and-gold swirls of tangible magic embedded into the soil, tethering the five kingdoms of Aksel to each other.

Videira   vee-dair-uh

The sacred vine of life is a sentient being that produces large green budding pods that bloom at the change of each season. The pods contain an infant child, known as the species called elf.

Marked Ones   markt wuhnz

Species or creatures endowed with extraordinary powers. They are gifted by the *Creator*, and it is still a mystery as to how they are chosen. They first came in abundance; now, their existence is rare.

Meir   may-eer

A luminescent orb sent directly from the vine during the changing of seasons. It floats to the various doorways inside the elven villages with a lantern on their doorpost, signaling to the vine that the particular household is ready for parenthood. Once at the chosen doorway, it leads the expecting couple back to the *Videira* ceremony grounds, where it is absorbed into a pod—the pod then blooms, revealing the elven infant to the parents.

Pod   pawd

Large green buds connected to the *Videira*. They bloom at the changing of each season with the assistance of absorbing the *Meir*.

Gavinhas   gah-veen-yahs

The whisps of light radiating from a being's aura. It is one's lifeline to the *Ligação Mágica* and their existence. It is a living creature or species ability to pass from this world to the next after death—what one would refer to as a soul.

Aura   or-uh

The energy encompassing each individual.

Mãe   ma-ee

A mother figure in the elven culture.

Papa   pah-puh

A father figure in the elven culture.

Xodó   show-doh

The current written language in the Elvish culture.

Reinos   ray-nohs

The spoken language used by all species in the five kingdoms of Aksel for communication.

Grato Amizade   grah-toh ah-mee-zah-jee

The holiday and celebration of the friendship and union between the kingdoms of Erebus and Alun.

Breeders of Thereon   bree-ders ov thay-run

Also referred to as *Breeders*, they were once dragons—now shrouded in dark magic, their souls corrupted by greed and a desire for power, were cut off from the *Ligação Mágica* by the *Creator*. They are bound to the blackened soil of Adara by an ancient spell cast by the monarchs of all five kingdoms before they fell. In order to hunt *Marked Ones*, they have found a way around the special by creating soulless creatures to do their bidding.

Thereon   thay-run

Soulless creatures derived from any species are created by their *Breeders* and are consumed by parasitic dark magic. These beasts hunt the *Marked Ones* and bring them back to their creators.

(Ah, I see you looking. You can't fool me and your wondering eyes. Certain words have been excluded from Book Two's glossary to prevent major plot reveals. Nice try, you sneaky minx.)

MAGIC SPELLS & INFORMATION

Spell Casting Explained:
There are three requirements necessary in order to cast a spell.
First, the caster must speak the language of Reinos, which is currently
recognized by all species and cultures within the five kingdoms.
Second, the being must be within range of the *Ligação Mágica*, the origin
of all enchanted magic.
Third, a source of friction is necessary to ignite the spell into existence—a
finger snap is most commonly used.

All three of these actions must coincide with one another for a basic spell to work. All beings and creatures are able to cast a spell, but it is deemed not wise. The *Creator* is always watching, and it is a bad omen to use the magic source if it is not out of necessity.

Only *Marked Ones* have the ability to use gifted powers from the *Creator*; it is not to be confused with magic.

Spells Used & Their Definitions:

Puero- to disappear; this spell is most commonly used for cleaning up small spills and messes.

Liguero- for speed; the elven species use this spell to pick up the pace when traveling through the dense forest of Alizeh.

Fogoe- to heat; can bring forth flames to a fire or simply warm a bubble bath.

Fria- to cool; you can freeze your dinner to save for a later time or chill your delicious pastry from the local baker.

Escureo- to cloak or disguise; used to conceal one's identity.

Escudo Preso Gavinhas- an intricate spell derived from the werewolf species, used to mask their soul's presence to outsiders.

You are allowed to feel. Let me say that again. *You. Are. Allowed. To. Feel.* You were *never* too much. You are a beautiful river of emotions, and you must find your people who will help guide you back to the sea, rather than leading you aimlessly; this will result in your evaporation. And you are worth so much more than that; you deserve a happy ending, my love.

Prologue

They were ethereal beings, with eyes born from stars that reflected the vast galaxies, each face carved from pure divinity. Flecks of gold were brushed upon their skin, resembling the cosmos along the various shades of reverent souls.

Their spirits were made flesh, and the celestial's hope gifted a vessel.

In response, a sudden pulse emerged from deep within the soil and traveled up to their core, where evil sprouted roots, taking on a physical form. For when something is born of light, an equal exchange is made; darkness gives birth in her shadows.

PART ONE

Chapter One

Sayah

The night's cool breath tickled my skin as goosebumps dispersed up and down the length of my arms. I was numb from the waist down, the frigid ocean water lapping at my sides before traveling the short distance to the shoreline. The sand was a piercing white; the flakes of snow blended into the scenery effortlessly. If I was not in this terrible predicament, I would have been enraptured by the stark contrast of the shadows of night illuminated by nature's tender kiss of death.

A numb pain radiated from my abdomen, blood swirling and mixing with the ink-colored sea. I grimaced, my gaze flickering up to the view of familiar uniforms that stood in an unwavering circle. The army of elves had positioned themselves strategically, swarming in the sand where the sea and land converged. My weary face was mirrored in their pointed blades.

The moon's calm reflection on the water's surface caught my attention as its white iridescence was stained crimson.

Frozen in my fury, I flexed my fingers. Their betrayal cut deeper than the darkest of trenches in the untouched sea, sharper than a thousand swords forged to fight the ghastly *Breeders of Thereon*. Those vile, corrupted dragons had been my sole enemy until I discovered my kingdom's true intentions. I scowled at the faces of Alizeh's soldiers; their distinct features burned into the labyrinth of my mind. The look of contempt and fear embedded in the harsh lines that came with war, with knowing death by name.

I disregarded the throbbing pain, the wound caused by the ringleader of the heartless *Thereon*. He had taken his sword moments before, slicing through the thick wool as if it were made of butter. *Mãe's* coat was torn in the battle; my sole heirloom stained with blood, the red liquid spreading like a plague across the blue fabric.

A part of me that I had yet to face awoke in my rage, the piece of me I was mortified to bring back into the light. This immense, fiery ball of anger burst through the walls of my control; the walls I had built over a lifetime of shame and guilt, for being brought into this world with such a horrendous gift. My rage was born the day *Mãe's* soul departed from this world and left for another. The festering negative energy merged with my power, boiling over and seeping out of my fingertips into existence. Before my rite of passage, my gift to siphon energy from any living entity had not been visible to anyone other than Ornella, my twin. But after touching the

Videira to be blessed by the sacred vine, my powers had awoken to their full extent.

My vision was enhanced, and I could see the details of the snowflakes that drifted to the sand, their brilliance reflecting the moonlight. I stepped toward the men as another wave crashed against my back, close to knocking me off balance. The blood loss was beginning to affect my physical state, yet the desire for revenge kept me upright. The soldiers cowered on their knees, their forest green uniforms disheveled, and the whites of their eyes widened as I drew near. My black wisps of power flowed out into the open, constricting around their *Gavinhas* like a snake squeezing the life out of its prey. The soft, ample tendrils of light encircling each being's aura dimmed in my grasp. I siphoned not only energy; their souls were mine for the taking.

Pleas for forgiveness fell on deaf ears as my craving for vengeance was all-consuming.

The moon was bright overhead, shining its radiant light onto the unfolding scene. The land's tangible magic was active; the illuminated green and gold swirls were a double-edged sword. I refused to pull from the magic here, even if it taunted me with its ease; how effortless it would be to cast a spell and escape imprisonment. However, the risk of synchronizing myself with one of the soldiers would not be worth jeopardizing my location in the future.

I would sooner perish as a free soul than lose sovereignty over my own thoughts.

The snowfall grew in intensity, catching on the unforgiving wind, temporarily shielding my vision of the soldiers here to arrest me for a crime

I did not commit. The situation grew dire; my legs were stiff from being submerged in the frigid sea.

Images of Ornella's face flashed across my mind, her white hair whipping in the wind as she was carried onto the enemy's vessel. Her choked cries rang fresh through my ears, numbing any compassion left inside my heart, now solid as stone. *Foolish elves.* They had been *right there*, watching as a *Marked One* was stolen in the midst of a celebration. Creatures cloaked in the parasitic magic had laid their grimy hands on her, whose only crime was to be fated to me. Their black sails had faded into the horizon, taking the last of the day's sun and warmth.

How dare they ignore my sister after all she has done—her pleas for help in her time of need.

For three hundred and twenty-five lunations, we had been under lock and key by the elders and priests who ruled our kingdom within the shadows of the picturesque landscape. Ornella willingly came to the aid of every elf in Alizeh without hesitation from the instant she was deemed old enough to leave the cottage unattended. She used her powers to give energy until she had none left for herself, draining her happiness at the expense of everyone else's peace.

And now, the kingdom of Alizeh had abandoned her.

I clenched my fists, heat rising to my cheeks. They abandoned me long ago, and my ability to siphon energy morphed me into a monster in their twisted perceptions.

It's time that I show them all what it truly means to fear a Marked One. If it is a monster they want, I am more than willing to oblige.

Another gust of wind slashed at my bare skin, drying my tears on my cheeks. *No more. No longer will I let the elves cast me aside and condemn me to a life of fear and helplessness.* Determined, I extended my arms and released my clasped hands to reveal another wave of untapped potential originating from my core. A plethora of black tendrils licked the air, eager to expand across the earth in search of more life so that they may claim its energy as their own. I glanced down at my palms and realized that I was shaking.

For my entire life, I was told to hide away this part of me, bury it deep inside, and never reveal it to others. The elders and priests deemed me too harmful and refused to let me explore my gift and its strength. Visions of my childhood plagued my memory; the judgmental eyes of my peers bore into my back as I walked the streets of the Woodlands. I felt them even now, the weight of their stares never leaving me. That feeling had sunk its claws deep into my flesh, traveling straight to my heart. It was an invisible open wound, a struggle, and a burden to accept. And underneath all the anger, I felt shame.

This is who I am at my center, at the bare bones of my existence.

Movement flashed in the corner of my eye, and I naturally tensed. A soldier lunged in my direction, his sword extended. My body swerved, narrowly missing the attack as I awkwardly stumbled forward in the shallow depths.

He was going to hurt me... The disbelief was visible in my features, my mouth agape as I stared at the strange man, gathering to compose himself in the sand.

The shock was replaced with hatred, as it contorted my features, a snarl in its place.

To save myself, the rage bottled inside instinctively poured out of my core in retribution. Whatever hesitation I had vanished as I syphoned the elven army's *Gavinhas*, the essence of who they were, *their souls*.

Chapter Two
Nox

Her beauty was haunting. She stood like a pillar waist-deep in the current, snow clinging to her fair skin. Her halo of raven locks moved with the wind; she was an omen glowing beneath the full moon.

Sayah was dangerous; I did not deny myself this fact. And yet I was drawn to her like a moth to a flame, my feet stumbling on the dry sand as I sprinted down the embankment to reach the water's edge.

Alizeh's army surrounded her on Erebus' shoreline, the soldiers crumpling to their knees as her power took form. Tendrils of black extended outwards from her figure in all directions as they searched the sandy beach, on the hunt for all energy and life. Some of her power clung to the soldiers' *Gavinhas,* the light wisps writhing outside their dim auras. A look of horror was plastered across their features, the elves' fear exposed as their swords shook in their hands, pointed directly at the threat.

I needed to reach Sayah before she acted solely on her emotions; she had never taken a life, and I wanted to keep her from experiencing that regret.

My breath was visible in the cold, and I clenched my jaw as my canines protruded from my mouth. I could feel the call of my ancestors, distinct beneath the moon's warm glow. The urge to fight was uncontrollable as claws instinctively released from my hands, muscles tensing in anticipation. A low growl erupted from deep within my chest.

I could smell her blood; she was wounded.

A tidal wave of guilt pierced my thoughts, forming a knot in the pit of my stomach. I had only protected one of the *Marked Ones* and left her sister vulnerable to both mental and physical attacks. That day on the vessel with Sayah, I should have cast the *Escudo das Almas* spell over Ornella, too. I did not mask her *Gavinha's* presence to outside invaders. The *Thereon* and Alizeh's army found us using the *Ligação Mágica,* connecting their souls' wavelengths to the sister who already had a strong connection with the elders and priests in their village. The ugly reality would eat away at me for this critical choice that changed our fate.

My infatuation with one sister led to the capture of the other.

Even in the cast of the shadows, my heart ached at the sight of her tear-stained cheeks. My markings hummed with electricity in response, and the orbs of light moved up and down my skin. I never told her what it meant, who she was to me. My tendrils of light had matched with hers, a rare occurrence for any werewolf. I didn't want to scare her away; we had met under strained circumstances. Maybe I shouldn't have kept it a secret.

My soul remembered her from a past life.

Why remained a mystery, but I noticed that my markings would react whenever she showed extreme emotion. She moved me in ways I could not explain, and regardless of the consequences, I knew this much: Sayah was a precious jewel I refused to let go of.

As I approached, the green and gold wisps swirled around her feet, the land's magic responding to the scene unfolding on the coastline. Even from this distance, my tethered soul felt her alluring tug.

Just being near her when she was in this uncontrollable state was a risk.

But I *knew her*, the young woman plagued by the powers gifted by the *Creator*. Her black irises were usually a misty grey, the color of winter's morning sky, just before the sun crested the horizon. Her laugh was harmonious, a product of her musical background. She had delicate, long fingers that danced across the ivory and ebony keys, her raw emotions vulnerable to all who would listen. The being before me was strikingly confident with a fiery temper, yet gentle with those she cared for. The *Creator* chose her specifically, and she bore the burden of such an immense power for a reason.

Sayah had a pure soul, fierce and unwavering. Those with weak foundations at their core trembled in her presence.

A monster in their eyes, she is the embodiment of all that is decent in mine.

And I hadn't dared express these thoughts. Regret formed a lump inside my throat as I advanced in haste. I dodged the elven soldiers that cowered below on the sand, nearly colliding with the woman who had enraptured my being since our first encounter.

In one fell swoop, my legs were submerged in water as I steadied my balance. The smell of blood was concentrated near her abdomen, where the red liquid pulled to the surface of her coat. Cradling her against my chest, my arms wrapped around her slender figure. I fought against the immense pull of her power, now draining my *Gavinhas*, threatening to end not only this life but also my ability to be reincarnated in the next.

"*Sayah*," I crooned, dipping my head into her raven hair. "*Come back to me.*"

She tensed, steadfast in her rage.

My hands cupped her heart-shaped face, and I knelt in the seawater, gazing upwards.

"*My Jewel*," I whispered, barely audible over the rhythmic waves meeting the shore. "You have every right to be angry. You have every right to scream into oblivion and take revenge on those who have wronged you for so many lunations." Searching her face, I paused, and Sayah's eyes darted to mine, filled with hurt. "But using all your strength now will leave none to rescue Ornella."

She blinked, absorbing my words.

"They're here...for *me*," Sayah croaked, fresh tears forming as her irises faded from black to grey. "Not for Ornella; they didn't come to save her. They are accusing *me* of attacking the elves on the day of our ceremony. Alizeh blames *me* for the deaths of women and children—*Mãe's death.*" Her anguish was evident in the raw emotion stemming from her voice as it grew in volume.

A sob escaped from deep within her chest, and I stood in time to catch her from collapsing into the ocean below.

My attention flickered between her and Alizeh's soldiers, who rose to their feet as I hugged her limp body against mine. Her black wisps of power withdrew back into her petite frame. It felt as though a weight had been lifted off my chest, now that my life was not in danger. I growled, angling her away from the men staring daggers at her in my arms. Sayah's breathing was ragged, and she winced as I adjusted her carefully.

Good. She could still feel pain, and that meant I still had time.

The outstretched black wisps of her power vanished from sight and retreated into her core as she lost consciousness.

"Hand her over to us; she belongs in the possession of the kingdom of Alizeh," one of the soldiers stated, his voice trembling.

My eyes darted between the jewel in my arms and the man, and I smirked at his claim.

"It appears she is, in fact, *in mine*—although Sayah is no being's possession." The words left my mouth with a cutthroat edge.

Alizeh's military formed a tight circle, unsheathing their weapons in unison. The snowfall was thick as I squinted at their pointed blades. I took count of the soldiers—there were at least thirty or so men that I would have to fight through while holding Sayah's unconscious body in my arms.

I needed a distraction.

"What crime has she committed? Sayah is not responsible for the recent attack on Alizeh." I cleared my throat; my voice pierced the air over the sounds of the ocean waves. "It was the *Thereon's* doing."

Their swords did not falter, and the soldier who had addressed me previously stepped forward, his confidence returning as his boots touched the lapping water.

"Sayah, daughter of Aster, is being charged for a separate crime." His declaration was low and even. "She attacked a fleet of soldiers deployed from the city of Ascelin to aid our troops at the *Videira*."

He hissed and clenched his jaw, looking directly at her. "Countless lives were lost *because of her*."

I paused, studying her crown of soft raven hair before meeting his gaze—pure hatred reflected inside the soldier's hazel eyes. I skimmed the elves encompassing me, and they all had the same look cast about their sharp features. They hated Sayah.

Giving her up to these pompous, pointy-eared blowhards was never an option.

I didn't believe a word of the garbage they spewed. The kingdom of Alizeh would lie, cheat, and kill to regain control over a *Marked One*. If I had learned anything useful from my father, it was not to trust another kingdom's military on their word alone.

My heart raced as I desperately searched the white landscape, shifting my weight from one foot to the other. *Where are Silas and Brom? Curse their thick skulls.* Both would receive an earful if I managed to avoid being captured.

My legs were starting to go numb, which would slow my escape. It seemed I was running out of options, so I began planning my escape route and calculating every move. Time was vital, and I needed to stop the bleeding from her wound.

"The way I see it," I raised a brow, my eye contact slowly making it around to every elven soldier, "the priests and elders are at fault for not warning their citizens of the threat several lunations ago when the *Thereon* began attacking the other kingdoms in search of *Marked Ones*."

I waded through the water, approaching the one who seemed to be their spearhead face to face, cradling Sayah far enough away from his grasp.

"You let your entire species down by keeping your loved ones in the dark. This is not the fault of one single being. This is the fault of a whole kingdom's heartless attitude and blatant ignorance."

His demeanor wavered, and his hazel eyes reflected disbelief. The tension between us was palpable, nearly as visible as the green and gold swirls of the *Ligação Mágica* dancing between our figures.

Snow clung to the soldier's eyelashes, hatred oozing out of him.

It was now or never. We would not see eye to eye or come to any agreement. That much was clear. Time stood still for several beats on Erebus' shore as I slowed my breathing, my focus honing in, waiting for the slightest distraction. My crew was nowhere to be found, and the panic in me began to rise as Sayah's body stopped shivering.

An abrupt sound of rushing water came up from behind, followed by a gush of wind spraying snow and sand at the army. They shouted, throwing up their arms to protect their eyes. A shadow was cast over the scene, the moonlight no longer visible among the sea of swords.

Flames burst through the air overhead, their cries dying underneath a deafening roar.

"*Wolf,*" a voice made of thunder reverberated through the air, splintering my ears. "*What have you done to my Marked One?*"

The relief was immediate as more fire scorched the night sky. She was the last being I expected to come to our rescue, her attitude as fickle as the weather. I relaxed my shoulders as she landed on the beach a few paces to my right.

A smile crept up my lips as the soldiers retreated toward their vessel, stumbling along the sand.

"Obsydora," I breathed, bowing my head in respect. Her blue scales looked startlingly white, a stark contrast between the moonlight and the snow reflecting off her reptilian form. She blew a remaining puff of smoke at the defeated men, her distaste for the elves evident before whipping her head to face me.

This dragon was starting to grow on me.

"The *Marked One* is without her other half," the cobalt-scaled lizard remarked, her head inclining to the north toward the kingdom of Adara. She made a clicking noise deep within her throat, speaking in her native tongue before lowering her neck as she inspected Sayah further. "Then there is no time to waste—bring her to me."

She didn't have to tell me twice. I climbed on top of her with ease, as she flattened her body to the ground for an easy acclimation. I then carried Sayah in my arms up Obsydora's spine. We rested where her neck and shoulders met, and I adjusted my jewel's figure in my lap. She was beautiful, even as her face twisted in pain, which caused my chest to tighten. *I will not let someone hurt Sayah like this again.*

As I held her there, Obsydora took to the starry sky, and I fought the urge to tell the dragon to fly faster; Sayah's steady heartbeat had already begun to flicker to a soft whisper.

Chapter Three
Sayah

My vision was shrouded in darkness, the air stagnant and eerily still. All thoughts had dissipated, and the wrath that had gripped my soul moments before was lost in the sea of nothingness. I was abruptly thrust forward at a blinding speed, moving through the cosmos. Iridescent light flashed around me, blazing my path and leading me to a room filled with stars, guiding the way to a river of vibrant color.

I gravitated to the body of water, mesmerized by its tranquil ripples flowing inside the void. Orbs of light were intertwined in the shimmering liquid as its stream continued into the vast interstellar chamber without a clear beginning or end.

"*It is not your time.*" A stark voice filled the space around my aura, sending shivers straight to the center of my existence. I turned and faced an entity made of light and magic. Its appearance resembled the elven species, though its entire composition was translucent. The being moved with a fluidity that frightened me. It circled me as I was frozen in place, its face twisted into a frown, causing my heart to race. They observed with an awareness that overwhelmed my senses. Their eyes, void of pupils, blinked as their brows creased, perplexed. "*Sayah, daughter of Aster. You should not be here.*"

The words entered my subconsciousness, giving birth without so much as an utterance from the figure's lips standing before me. It was a voice melded from life itself, blended from all sounds of nature.

My eyes widened, and I stumbled backward, comprehending *who* the being was.

The Creator.

I shook my head in doubt. There was no possible way that the *Creator* of this world would reveal themselves. Yes, I was a *Marked One,* but I had done nothing remarkable to be graced with their presence.

And then it moved, shifting its figure to that of an ogre as it approached the river, no longer facing my direction. Their massive hands reached into the shimmering liquid, plucking an orb from its contents. It held the glowing ball of light up close, examining its flickering fumes and multicolored sparks before gently releasing it back in the waterway.

"*Your lack of control is repetitive and uninteresting,*" they mused, staring out far beyond what I could see. Unease crept along my arms in the form of goosebumps as the *Creator* stood motionless for several beats.

And then they were at my side, taking the form of a fairy. Their wings, made of light, fluttered, creating an irritating buzzing sound. It reminded me of someone, but I couldn't recall who. I held my breath when they flew to my ear, sending a tingling sensation down my neck and spine.

"*Atone for your sins, my child.*"

"Sins? What sin have I committed?"

"*It is to be seen.*"

My eyes widened in disbelief, and I bit my cheek to help hold my tongue. "You're accusing me of committing a sin that has yet to happen? How can you be so sure of a decision I will make in the future?"

"*It is the same choice in every life I have blessed you with. But this is the last time.*"

The buzzing around my ears went quiet; the air around us grew still. A chill ran down my spine, and I hesitantly twisted my head around to peer behind me. The *Creator's* shape had begun to morph, their arms and legs disproportionate in size, as claws ripped from their fingers. Their figure grew as tall as the pines in Alizeh at lightning speed. I fell to my knees in fear, my body trembling as a massive predator flashed its fangs, drool dripping from its mouth. An animalistic scream was caught in the depths of my throat as the entity who breathed life into existence had taken on the form of a dragon and released a deafening roar.

Their flames melded into my tendrils of light and swallowed me whole.

Chapter Four

Sayah

No sound left my throat as I screamed; the burning sensation scorched my lungs, my tendrils of light engulfed in white flames. Visions of dragons covered in a black parasitic magic flashed across my vision; their canines protruded from their mouths, as drool dripped from their chins. The beast's auras were intense, blanketing a heavy weight on my chest. I could sense the corruption in their hearts, the desire for power visible in their reptilian irises. But then they were gone, and I was again left in a bitter darkness. Though brief, I knew the horrid sensation would haunt me in this life and the next. A chill ran up my spine, leaving the hair on my arms and neck at attention. My identity blurred inside the empty abyss, an afterthought of all that existed.

After several beats, a numbing pain pulsed in my abdomen, and an involuntary whimper left my lips.

"*Marked One,*" a booming voice rattled inside the void, shaking me. "*You must fight to stay. Do not take the easy path; the feeling of peace. Strength is forged in moments of difficulty, when the foundation of who you are is put to the ultimate test. And if not for you, fight for her. She needs you now more than ever.*"

She? Who is she? And who is speaking?

Flashes of color filled the emptiness, and a vision formed as emerald eyes crinkled with joy as they met mine. A beautiful woman with white waves cascading down her shoulders, which blended into the blurry background, stood a foot away. She was there, in the sun, moon, and stars. Her laughter was addictive, sending warmth to what was left of my shattered heart.

My focus shifted, and we were now inside a room filled with instruments. And I instantly knew if I could live inside a moment in time, this would be where I would reside. I wanted to linger here and feel the warmth of the sun that trickled in from the front window on my skin. This place was the epitome of peace. There was an irony in the fact that I sat in a room meant to be bursting with life's melodies and sound, yet all I wanted was to soak in the quiet. It was a comfortable place to be in, and my soul wedged itself between the eerily tranquil feeling, completely content. The familiarity of the quaint storefront was staggering, and I ran my fingers over the top of a grand piano, flicking away the accumulated dust. The same woman was seated at the bench, the light radiating from the open window soft on her rosy skin.

She patted the seat, her expression hopeful with a lingering question in her eyes.

I did not move; my feet were planted firmly on the wooden floor. My hesitation became a flat-out refusal, and panic twisted a knot in my stomach as a thin line formed on my lips, the blood draining from my skin. I was afraid, terrified of losing something precious the instant I recollected my thoughts.

White waves bounced as she squeezed her eyes shut and shook her head. The woman's features fell from disappointment.

"*Remember,*" she pleaded with me, the bench scraping across the floor as she stood. Her voice parted the persistent fog, and a song wafted through the space, caressing my ears.

I gravitated toward the music, which merged into the shimmering green and gold waves of magic, and they pulled me to something—no, *someone*.

The woman who had woven me into her orbit had vanished, and in her place was my own reflection. But there was an unfamiliar crease in my brow, a hardened look in my eye. I then gasped as my reflection turned away from me, placing the palms of her hands on a large vine, an iridescent light radiating from the massive stem.

She was touching the *Videira,* the sacred vine.

The flash of light dissipated as my eyes fluttered open, and I was met with the night sky. The stars were within reach as they fluttered by at a blinding speed. A chill ran down my arms as the sharp, cold air sliced at my exposed skin.

"She's awake," a man's voice broke the silence. The relief in his announcement was tangible, and my heart skipped a beat at the sound.

"Don't scare me like that again," he growled in my ear, and a name surfaced from the back of my mind.

"Nox." The word was but a whisper on my lips.

He pulled me close, cradling me against his chest. The world still moved at a staggering pace, and flashes of blue reflected off the surface below. My eyes trailed over his ragged appearance, the dark circles beneath his russet eyes prominent. His arm moved, and my focus shifted as the feeling of overwhelming guilt surfaced at the sight of the white scars that swirled up and down his forearm, distorting his tribal markings, a reminder of the pain I had inflicted on him for my recklessness with past decisions.

"Where are we?" I tried to tip my head forward to see, but an impenetrable gust of wind prevented me from turning.

"Obsydora is flying us to Alun." He caressed my cheek, brushing a few loose strands of hair behind my ear. "Don't worry for now. You must rest, Sayah." His resolve faltered, and only what I can describe as dread befell the werewolf's face.

Why is he looking at me with such pity and regret?

Ornella. A pang of realization ripped through me as I winced and clenched the fabric above my chest. *She was gone.*

My own flesh and blood. Fragmented memories flooded my consciousness; I recalled the fear in her emerald eyes as creatures cloaked in black carried her aboard a foreign ship before sailing away to Adara—the kingdom where only sorrow was born from its cursed soil. And atop that wretched land of fire and ash sat Mount Auberon, housing the *Breeders of Thereon:* Once dragons, disowned by their brethren after their souls became corrupt with an overwhelming desire for power.

They hunted *Marked Ones*, those gifted by the *Creator* with extraordinary powers. The five monarchs in Aksel had sentenced them using an ancient magic to wither away deep inside Auberon's caverns. But dragons were inherently cunning, as were the *Breeders*. And the vile abominations wouldn't let their severed ties with the *Creator* and the *Ligação Mágica* keep them from their desire for power; it consumed them whole.

The *Breeders* sent their morbid creations, the *Thereon*, out into the lands to do their bidding while simultaneously destroying all hope. To take *more* than life, a being's ability to reincarnate.

They were monsters made of rotten flesh and greed, and Ornella was their prisoner.

I fought the urge to cry, swallowing my feelings as I forced the lump back down my throat. All I did was make mistakes. So many vital choices were in my control that if I had made the right decisions, our lives would not have lost their former potential due to my inadequacies.

Our family would be living a quaint, uneventful, and extremely ordinary life in the Woodlands of Alizeh. *Mãe* would teach music lessons at her academy, and Ornella would be in the garden behind our cottage, gathering ingredients to try her best before failing yet again at cooking another supper.

If only I had stayed vigilant and protected her Gavinhas with the spell Nox had taught me.

The throbbing pain inside my chest kept me from speaking, and the ringing in my ears grew in intensity. Nox held me close, and I studied the tribal markings peeking out from his shirt and at his collarbone. The black swirls were glowing, and a sudden warmth spread through my limbs, my tensed muscles relaxing in response to the sensation. I had never been more grateful for his presence and willingness to comfort me in my darkest moments.

The wind suddenly whipped my hair across my face and skin, bringing me back to reality and reflecting the chaos brewing beneath it.

Chapter Five

Nox

I observed her there as I loomed just outside the doorway. Her black hair lay untouched against the white pillow, a stark contrast to the midnight strands of silk that framed her heart-shaped face. She had been unmoved since the day I brought her to the manor. Sayah was awake on the trip to Alun with Obsydora, but as soon as we landed, her eyes were shut and she was quiet.

The feeling of unease crept up my back and shoulders as her chest rose and fell with each steady breath. I couldn't shake the ominous feeling that she was suspended in time and only needed me to call to her gently for her to wake.

"Sayah's eyes will open soon; I can feel it," the high-pitched rasp originated from behind my ear. I didn't have to turn my head to know that Kazumi was there, her wings softly vibrating and stirring up the wind. A few pieces of my hair blew forward, untucked from the tight low bun I had secured this morning. When I didn't speak, she continued. "Your father is looking for you."

Heat flushed my skin at the mention of him, and I visibly grimaced. "What for?" I twisted to meet her black, beady eyes, her expression tight-lipped.

"You know what for," she stated before disappearing down the hall.

He sent her because he knew I wouldn't dare to yell at a fairy for fear of being cursed, that conniving snake. The smell of supper wafted from down in the dining room, where my crew impatiently waited for me to break the silence. I breathed a sigh, moving away from Sayah. Silas was the sole reason I would leave my jewel's side to greet my father; I refused to leave my friend alone with these blowhards for more than a few moments at a time.

My eyes lingered on her for another second before I involuntarily turned to follow behind Kazumi. The thought of Sayah trapped in a wakeless sleep still burdened my soul as I traced my fingers along the decorative walls and made my way to the banister at the end of the hall. I knew of another cursed with a similar fate, and I could not bear to let another be burdened with the same unfortunate consequence. I scoffed, crossing my arms. This beautiful mansion was nothing more than a cage; my father used all his power to keep me confined here at the vineyard.

It was my birthright, after all.

His booming voice reached me as soon as I descended the staircase. The low vibrations laced with anger were more recognizable than my own voice; I gritted my teeth before squeezing the railing one final time and making my way to the large wooden doors. I paused at the entrance, and my ears twitched. Hushed voices slipped beneath its cracks. For reassurance, I unbuttoned the top of my shirt to reveal more of the intricate black swirls that stopped just below my neck.

I wasn't a fool; I knew that his one weakness was *power*, and I needed every advantage that I could muster if I were going to endure yet another argument. It was the only reason he let me leave Alun in search of a cure for the *Thereon* and to rescue Tabitha. And I needed another ship with supplies, so I had to play nice tonight.

I straightened and flung the entrance open to make way for my grand appearance.

"Finally," my old man choked as he sat poised at the end of the long table, spilling his drink onto his lap. "And here I thought you wouldn't grace us with your presence on such an important occasion."

My focus immediately flickered to where his hand rested on Silas' shoulder. I instinctively clenched my jaw at the sight of it, not missing the strict squeeze of his hand before releasing his grip and flexing his fingers.

Silas was rigid, his golden irises unwavering under the pressure. The rest of our crew of misfits didn't know the extent of the trauma, the burden behind having no markings to signify strength.

The entire table was filled with family and guests, some of whom I did not recognize. The display of food was extravagant; it was enough sustenance to feed an entire army of soldiers. I nearly scoffed at the waste of goods for one ridiculous meeting with another clan.

Without hesitation, I pulled out a chair next to Silas, ignoring the seat next to my father and the random woman who sat adjacent to me. She had blonde hair, shaved on one side to display the black swirls that decorated her skull, and the other was adorned with several braids mixed into her waves that cascaded down her back. She had irises the color of honey, the sole soft part of her hardened exterior. It was obvious that she had been brainwashed into the ways of the four clans since birth. Her hopeful gaze met mine.

It took everything in me to hold back the recoil in my expression.

"And what occasion would that be?" I picked up the silverware and eyed the spread of delicious food, ignoring my father's glare. "Our homecoming, perhaps?" I said as I took a mouthful of roasted duck. The table had gone quiet, waiting for the tension in the room to ease before continuing their supper.

"I would have celebrated your homecoming if you had come back with something worth noting, Nox," my father spat from across the table, his words a tangled mess. "But instead, you sink one of my fleet ships, bring me a horde of dragons to find lodging for, *and* you manage to find a *Marked One*—but not the prize of the bunch, unfortunately."

I stabbed my fork into the wooden table and looked up in time to see him pointing a finger directly at me. "She's one of those cursed ones; she steals energy from life itself, son. And you brought *that beast* into our home." He slowly lowered his hand, and the blood that had rushed to the surface of his skin faded.

Everyone's attention rested on me, but I couldn't peel mine away from the sorry excuse that was my father. On the outside, I was a mirror image of him. We had the same long, brown locks; our brown skin was decorated with tribal markings. Even our eyes were the same russet color, swirling with determination. A few greys were now sprinkled in his beard and mane, and wrinkles had taken shape around his sharp features.

If only I had been blessed with my mother's amber eyes or tender smile.

I bit the inside of my cheek, blood boiling. "She's not cursed, and if you insult Sayah again, I'll show you what a beast *I* can be." My voice was even as I pushed my threat further by flexing my claws. When he made no advances, I casually grabbed a dinner roll from the basket. "Tell me what you want before I split this table in two."

So much for me playing it nice.

I felt a jolt from underneath the table, and Enid, from the left of me, curtly shook her head no. She kept me out of trouble most of the time, well, she and Silas. Leaning back in my chair, I crossed my arms above my head and used the extravagant dining table as a footrest. Brom, that burly ogre, had finally stopped gorging on his supper; his mouth was left gaping at what my father would call disrespect.

"I want you to meet your betrothed, Caelan, from the Iron Nightwalkers clan." The plastered grin across my father's face wiped mine clean off. "She is their strongest female warrior, and your pairing is most advantageous for both parties."

There was a ringing in my ear, alongside an uncontrollable urge to rip everything to pieces.

Jumping up from the table, I nearly knocked Silas out of his chair. "I thought we only mated from within the clan," I challenged, gripping the table's edge for support so I didn't try and rip his head clean off. "What was all that nonsense you ingrained into me as a child about keeping the lineage pure?" My gaze finally met Caelan's, and to my surprise, it was not shock that filled her features, but a knowing disdain.

So, the woman knew exactly what she was getting into after all.

"That's in the past; we are moving forward to create a better future." My father's awareness darted to a silver-haired man sitting at the table. His cunning eyes took in every inch of our messed-up relationship. He must be the chief of the Iron Nightwalkers—and Caelan's father.

A growl ripped from my throat. With Tabitha gone, our clan no longer had the unfair advantage of controlling the moon's energy. Being a *Marked One* seemed to be more of a burden than anything. If only my sister had not been blessed with such a gift by the *Creator*. She was a key player in my father's plan for success, and the other clans must now finally be aware of her kidnapping. The information would have leaked eventually, and so it was only a matter of time before the other blowhards discovered it and used it against us. This was how he planned to maintain power over the other three clans without a full-out war erupting, as his control was loose at the seams. He wanted Caelan, the daughter of Chief Bjorn, to be my chosen mate. Or, perhaps this was the Iron Nightwalker's direct attempt at power without resorting to fangs and claws. *Interesting.*

Regardless of whose motives this benefited most, that would not happen. I would lose my *Gavinhas* to the *Thereon* before I gave up my freedom to choose.

I released my grip on the table; the wood splintered and cracked from my tight grip. I sauntered around the dinner party, passing by my friends whose eyes bulged wide, all except Kazumi, who flew about the feast, completely content as she snacked on all the delicacies. That alone made the smirk playing along the edge of my lips grow wide as I towered over Caelan, still seated in her chair.

Her dipped-in-honey eyes were oddly placed inside the hostile, sharp-edged appearance of a warrior. It made me almost laugh—her innocent nature was smoke and mirrors.

"My heart belongs to another," I stated, my pulse accelerating. "And you would have me be your mate anyway, even if I were never to love you?"

She paused, calculating, her eyes never breaking away from mine.

"This isn't about *you* and your feelings. It's for the well-being of our clans. You could at least act like you had a proper upbringing," Caelan answered, turning back to the table and picking up her utensils. She ate the food on her plate without giving me a second glance.

"Nox!" my father roared, and I twisted my body to see his fangs and claws protruding. "How dare you talk to your mate in such a way! *You insolent brat*!" He lunged in my direction, and I dodged his advance. He clumsily took several plates, crashing to the floor, multiple dishes of food following suit.

"Phoenix, enough," Chief Bjorn barked, and his tone was the equivalent of a brewing storm. My father's head turned at the mention of his name, and he froze in place. "How did you expect him to react if you hadn't prepared him beforehand?" His stare flickered to mine, and unease crept up my neck.

My father's guest gestured with his arms out wide.

"He told me that you are trying to rescue Tabitha, your sister, from the *Breeders of Thereon* in Mount Auberon. Caelan will assist you." He gestured toward his daughter, whose terrible poker face had disappeared completely. She mouthed the words "*I will not*" at him, and he dismissed it with a wave of his hand. "We will tend to the *Marked One* while you two are away; you'll naturally spend time with one another, and a bond will form. Caelan has been sent on many missions; she is an asset on any battlefield."

Before I could speak another thought, she interjected.

"I agreed for him to be my mate in *name only*, Chief Bjorn." Spite oozed from her lips, and I was now bearing witness to her true nature. "I refuse to leave the kingdom of Alun for a lost cause. All that is left of his sister now is a walking corpse." She glared at me, her expression stern. "If the *Thereon* took her, she is no longer with us."

With my fists clenched, I met her intensity as my nails dug into my palms.

"She is not one of those corrupted monsters; I can feel her through the *Ligação Mágica*. Her *Gavinhas* are still intact." I countered, jutting my jaw forward in defiance. Our stalemate grew increasingly awkward, neither of us willing to budge.

A young maiden burst through the dining hall's door in that instant, shattering the tension.

"She's awake!" The girl stumbled forward, almost tripping over a chair. "*The Marked One;* her eyes opened!" Her movements were erratic as she scanned the area, and after a few seconds, I recognized her as my cousin, Odette. Her head of auburn ringlets bobbed as she scampered forward, not minding the mess of broken glass. She made it to my side, breathless, grabbing my forearm. "Nox—she's asking for you."

Chapter Six

Qunella

The *Breeder's* face was inches from mine, his breath reeking of ash and rotting flesh. Smoke rose from his nostrils and traveled between the rusted metal bars, unaffected by the blue ancient magic encompassing my prison. The parasitic magic that clung to his crimson scales crawled up and down his spine, the black entity moving of its own volition. His sharp, serpentine eyes examined every inch of me; the strength of his aura flooded the space as I cowered against the back of my cage.

"I've waited *centuries*." The *Breeder's* declaration shook the elevated caverns, our cages threatening to fall to the depths below. "Over thousands of lunations." His massive figure consumed the area surrounding my cage, hiding the other prisoners from view.

I could not articulate a single thought or move from my frozen position. Fear had taken hold of my body. He was the epitome of hell rising from the depths of despair to greet me. There was no other way to describe the feeling of horror his presence planted in my heart. This *Breeder* showed no signs of empathy or forgiveness like Fraener or Obsydora, the dragons I had met on the Isles of Cadogan, where they were hiding from the destruction of their species. No, he had morphed entirely into what I considered to be the origin of nightmares; the true meaning of what it meant to be a monster.

The black inky magic encompassing the corrupted beast started to inch toward me across the iron base, and an instinctive whimper escaped my lips.

Bakunax was his former name, and he was indeed the shell of a dragon—his scales were blood-red; even after all this time inside Mount Auberon, they glimmered without light. But what was most frightening was not his size or razor-sharp canines bared in my direction, but his eyes.

One glimpse into the depths of his irises, and you knew he was no longer the same as his kindred. The soul trapped beneath all the corruption peered into my own, snagging onto every flaw that existed within me in an instant. He made me feel bare, my depravities overflowing out into the open, exposed for all to see.

"Only those who are weak-natured believe those who are powerful to be monsters." His words shook my prison as he reflected my thoughts. I sucked in a narrow breath, limbs trembling.

Can he read my thoughts?

"Our species was among the first to walk these lands—my origins are quite pure." His reptilian eyes blinked, almost making contact with the rusted metal. "I do not need to read your mind to know that you view me as a *Breeder of Thereon*, the name given to me after my brethren disowned me."

"H-how are you doing that?" I squeaked, clearing my throat. My voice was hoarse from the many moons I had spent screaming for help on the *Thereon's* ship.

"I have lived long enough to know what you *Marked Ones* are thinking." He scoffed, his irises retracting. "I have been a part of these lands before they were kingdoms, before *Marked Ones* existed. You have no clue about your origins. You are not pure, but you and your other half will be enough."

The beast's head snapped in the direction of his army, the soulless *Thereon* dancing around their masters, creating a blasphemous ritual rising from the depths of all greed and desire. Other *Breeders* were gathered in the center, the dark magic consuming them, creeping up the length of their spine in harsh, jagged movements.

"Foolish creatures—do not celebrate!" Bakunax's warning grew in volume, shaking the caverns as several stones came loose, echoing as they bounced off the walls. "A great war is coming; now is the time to rest. Absorb the power transferred into your veins and fulfill your purpose."

The army of *Thereon* shrieked with joy, howling like rabid animals as they waited eagerly in anticipation.

Bakunax leveled his stare with mine, and a clicking noise came from the back of his throat. He was speaking in the dragon dialect. "The final *Marked One* will come for you, and that will be the beginning of the end."

His hot breath skimmed across my cage to meet me, and my body revolted. The last sentence whispered off his lips was in the language of *Reinos,* the language that all creatures shared, so all the *Marked Ones* in their cells could understand.

The end was coming, and Sayah would either be our liberator or our undoing.

Chapter Seven

Tabitha

The most recent captive trembled in the cage next to mine, her eyes glued to the back of Bakunax as his massive figure slithered off to tend to his flock of *Thereon*, impatiently waiting for him on the limestone floor. She seemed unbothered by the chains as she spiraled into despair. The bewildered look set in her features led me to such a conclusion.

"Do not mind him or what anyone else says to you here," I instructed as fear shuddered through her slender frame. Waves of white framed her heart-shaped face; her emerald eyes and sharp nose felt oddly familiar. "I've been here long enough to know that they will use fear as a means of control.

We ultimately are nothing more than a tool, waiting to be plucked from our prisons for their use."

The young woman kept her back pressed against the bars, tears streaking down her cheeks.

"How long?" she whispered, lip quivering.

The pause between us lasted several beats as I forced myself to think. I had been avoiding my memories shortly after arriving. Hope for escape had unraveled in my stay here, as it did with the other *Marked Ones*. We hadn't been permitted the option to converse with one another; a man with multicolored eyes had made sure of that. I clenched my teeth, brushing some of the soot off my skin, wincing at the bruises underneath the shackles on my wrists. Memories were more painful than any amount of physical pain I had endured while trapped here.

I eventually gulped, a lump in my throat forming. "Long enough."

Long enough to forget how the sun felt on my skin, the wind's gentle rustling of my hair, and the scent of the grapes ready to be harvested from their clusters back at the vineyard. The taste of a home-cooked meal was all but familiar, and a face flashed across my mind, causing me to catch my breath.

His golden eyes were kind, and his smile genuine as he held out his hand. The scar that ran diagonally up his left brow had begun to fade white, and I missed every inch of who he was.

Silas always felt like *home*, like the summer rain cooling your skin after a hot day, a sip of hot cocoa on a cold winter's night. He loved me for who I was, not for the abilities I possessed. I found his calm and quiet nature to be exactly what I desperately needed.

"What will happen to us?" she urged. The woman fully faced me, her emerald eyes wide with anticipation. Her question had brought me out of my trance, and I pressed my lips in a thin line, scanning the other cells dangling from the cavern's ceiling.

"Bakunax and the other *Breeders* need us for our gifts. He will drain us of our powers, and we will die either by his hand or by the army of *Thereon*." I raised a brow, wiping the sweat off my forehead. "Either way, our future is grave." A group of *Thereon* turned their heads our way, drool falling from their chins. It was shocking to realize that they had once been a different species entirely, with thoughts, dreams, and plans of their own. Now, they were ghastly monsters cloaked in the black oozing magic, void of any tendrils of light. I couldn't help but feel a twinge of sorrow when looking at the soulless beasts, as this would be the last life they ever lived, the last of their existence.

Redemption had abandoned them, along with the *Creator*.

"Grave indeed," she replied, lying in a fetal position facing the soft glow from deep within the depths of Mount Auberon.

I knew the light was not a light at all, but rather the masses of gold and gemstones gifted from the long-forgotten monarchs. It was initially the source of my courage, the will to fight for freedom. I had been ignorant in thinking it was the way out of this dark abyss, the exit that I would eventually escape from.

I kept quiet, pulling my knees into my chest as I examined her pointed ears and the back of her head. Her soft waves clashed with the rusty iron floor; she reminded me of a rabbit who had wandered into a fox's den. Naive, beautiful, and foolish.

No, I wouldn't tell her. Maybe that hope in her heart would last a little longer, giving her a reason to pray for better days.

A sob suddenly rose from my chest, the noise awkward as I tried to cover it with a fit of coughs. With my head tilted upward, I squeezed my eyes shut, unable to hold in the few tears that ran down my face.

I thought of my brother back home, his features hardened from life's trials and tribulations since he was a young boy.

Nox had been right, after all. Ignorance truly was bliss.

Chapter Eight

Sayah

A gentle hum grew in volume, tickling my ears, and a calming sensation spread throughout my limbs. I tried to move my fingers, but all I could manage was a slight twitch in my hands. The haze over my memory lingered like the morning fog in spring. *Where was I?* All I could recall was a deep feeling of regret. A strong aroma of lavender interrupted my train of thought and filled my lungs. After several deep inhales of the comforting smell, I awoke inside an unfamiliar chamber. The lighting was dim, except for the sun's rays illuminating the floor-length curtains draped over a partially opened window.

A girl hovered over me, brushing my hair behind my ears as she softly sang a lullaby. Her auburn curls shimmered even in the shadows; hazel eyes grew wide with shock as they met mine, and she instantly moved for the doorway.

"Wait." I caught the sleeve of her dress, her figure hesitating at my touch. "Where am I?" I rasped, my voice hoarse.

"The kingdom of Alun." Her cautious response was stated matter-of-factly. The gown she wore swayed at her ankles, catching on a breeze sneaking in through the window. We were suspended there for several seconds until I released my hold on her garment.

My brows furrowed, and I chewed on my index finger's cuticle, perplexed by the events leading to my arrival in a completely different kingdom than I remembered.

"Why am I here? Where is Ornella?" Alarmed, I sat up, dread taking shape as my eyes scanned the room.

"Don't sit up!" The girl's features were lined with worry as she moved to my side, softly squeezing my hand in hers. As she pressed a damp cloth to my forehead, I examined the sharpness of her eyes, her tendrils of light waving brightly around her aura. She acted as if she had done this many times, often caring for the sick or wounded. And all I could think was that she was awfully young to know how to tend to those recovering from injuries or illness.

Something was terribly wrong, and my sister's absence was deafening in the girl's silence. And then it erupted—a hot, festering pain in my abdomen. I gasped, hands instinctively holding my side as I fell back on the mattress.

The girl reminded me of Ornella, who had been forced to tend to the sick and wounded from a young age. In the awkward pause, I lifted my shirt to see the dressings wrapped around my torso.

"Is there someone in charge that I can speak to?" I was now the cautious one, staring up at the ceiling. There were shapes carved into the wood purely for aesthetic, familiar swirls that reminded me of something. *Someone.*

She cleared her throat, snatching her hand away from my forehead. "I am practically an adult; my one hundredth and seventieth lunation is a few moons away. I'll be able to enter the arena and earn my first tribal marking." Her delicate arms rose in the air as she inspected every freckle and hair.

Tribal markings. A hazy image of a man's arm covered in white swirling scars traveling up his forearm flashed across my mind. I squinted at the designs directly above me, taunting my fuzzy memory. The blurry image I recalled then connected with the pattern, like a puzzle piece fitting into place.

I took a deep inhale, and a sharp pain radiated from my skull as I remembered it all at once. The *Videira's* translucent interior upon arrival at the ceremony grounds, and the multicolored orbs weaving their way throughout the sentient being. How on the day of our rite-of-passage, the sacred vine did not acknowledge our presence immediately, and the painful few seconds it took before our souls connected and a luminescent light spread from the tips of its canopy to mine and my sister's limbs. It was from that moment on that our lives had been altered, our powers fully awakened, and the turmoil that ensued stemmed from that single event.

My neck and cheeks flushed as I recalled my sister's face disappearing aboard one of the *Thereon's* black vessels. The soulless beasts had taken her hostage—I needed to know if someone had saved her. *How long had it been since I last saw her on Erebus' shore? A few moons?* I couldn't imagine her having to go through such a horrendous event alone; her heart had always been fragile. One small crack from shattering under the illusion she was strong enough to endure everything on her own.

"Where's Nox?" I bit the inside of my cheek, unable to mask the desperation as I pleaded. "Where is he? May I see him?"

Her hazel eyes widened once more, an awareness dawning across her features. She gripped both of my hands in hers, and a wave of authority shook from her thin frame. "You do not move so much as an inch, or you'll hear it from me." The girl then lifted my garment to examine my dressings, a bright red blush heating my face and neck. "If you move, and mess up all the hard work I've done nursing you back to health, you'll have to face *me* head-on in the arena." Her lips cracked into a smile as she instantly let go, darting for the door. I observed as auburn curls bounced out of sight, and I slumped back into the bed, irritated, but my heart was pounding all the same.

I held it together until the sound of her footsteps were faint against the ringing in my ears, and my composure collapsed. Guilt surged through my chest, tears clinging to my eyelashes as a painful lump formed in my throat.

She knew.

The girl's face when I asked where Ornella was—there was a deep sorrow in her eyes. I gripped the sheets between my fists as I fought the overwhelming urge to weep into the echoes of the unfamiliar room, bringing my despair into the world around me as I mourned reality.

My sister was my twin, our bond deeper than most. Our souls had been synchronized from the beginning of our creation, and I did not need to cling to our kingdom's tangible magic to know that she was nowhere near Alun.

I had been sleeping in a clean, comfortable bed while Ornella was in the kingdom of Adara, imprisoned by the *Breeders of Thereon*.

Chapter Nine
Nox

I couldn't get to her fast enough; my heart was pounding out of my chest as I sprinted past my father's house guests and the crew. My soul carried me to hers, the yearning in my heart orchestrating a veil between everyone else and our destined tendrils of light. The world around me was a blur, and I honed in on the one being whom I'd been desperately praying to awaken.

She didn't need to forgive me—just having her full consciousness back in this world was more than enough.

Why had I left her when Ornella went missing? Looking back on it now, I hadn't the slightest clue. When it came to Sayah, I found myself at her beck and call. She had urged me to leave, but the fact still stands that both sisters were my priority.

My brow furrowed as I sprinted up the staircase. *Tabitha would have reacted appropriately in that situation. She would have known not to leave the last Marked One alone without protection.*

What would my sister say to me if she were here? An image of her leaning against the wall, arms crossed, as she shook her head, her strawberry blonde ringlets bouncing in tune with her disappointment. She was younger than I, and yet as we grew, everyone around us began to think she was the older sibling. Part of the reason for the confusion was that she became a mother figure to me after our mom's tragic incident.

Tabitha would have handled the mission the right way, not letting her feelings dictate her decisions. Even now, that was what moved me forward. This, and my guilt. It was my fault they were in this mess; I had taken both twins without their permission from the kingdom of Danu to use them as bait, and I did not consider the repercussions. My excuse at the time was that they were in danger and I was also saving them from being captured by a *Thereon.*

But Sayah had made it blatantly clear that it was not the path she would have chosen for herself; that my crew and I had not given her and Ornella the ability to choose.

I felt just as wicked as the elders in Alizeh, as devious as my father. Those who ruled the five kingdoms of Aksel tried to control the *Marked Ones,* without giving them the autonomy they deserved.

The repercussions for these actions, I was certain, would be the very end of me.

I didn't remember how I ended up at her bedside; I was there, staring at her wide-eyed, beautiful face. Words were caught in my throat, and I stood there frozen like a fool until she spoke.

"Where's Ulfred?" were unexpectedly the first words off her lips. Sayah's focus drifted from mine to the left of me, and I partially turned my head to the audience lingering at the doorframe.

Enid was there, her features fighting between relief and something else. The ogress's clothes were disheveled, her usual low ponytail loose, and pieces of brunette hair framed her strong jaw. Brom, her brother with similar features, was next to her. His chocolate eyes were filled with tears as a sob wracked his giant frame. He was not afraid to express his emotions for all to see, and I respected him immensely for it.

I felt a hand rest on my shoulder, and Silas was there, too, staring intently at Sayah. He pressed his lips together and nodded once to me, and then his attention met the rest of the onlookers.

"Let's give her a minute to regain her thoughts before we bombard her. Nox, since she asked for you, why don't you stay and answer any questions she has?" Silas's brow arched, and my shoulders relaxed. He knew how to read a room. My best friend patted my back as he walked past, pausing momentarily to give Sayah a small smile. "We are relieved to see that you are awake. When you are ready, we will come to say hi." His voice was gentle, as if he were coaxing an injured animal.

They all shuffled down the corridor and out of sight, apart from Enid. She remained at the entrance, her lips pursed. After several seconds of Sayah staring intently at her, she sighed, and her hand fell from the doorframe. "I'll bring you breakfast in the morning." The ogress turned her heel and went opposite the others toward the living quarters.

I half-smiled, turning my full attention to Sayah. "Food is her love language. She missed you."

A light flickered in her pools of grey, tears merging in their corners.

"Ulfred stayed in Erebus. He bought us the time we needed to escape Alizeh's army." I stated the facts, fighting off the emotion that threatened to invade my calm demeanor. "He wanted to be here, Sayah. But he chose to sacrifice time with you, so that you would have time. Freedom."

A weighted intensity in the room grew with her shocked stare. Her hands clutched her blanket as if they were the only thing that tethered her to reality.

The old werewolf was her *mãe's* partner, and the man whom she was sure, in her eyes, was the father figure she had been denied. With *Mãe* gone, he was a long-forgotten wish that had unexpectedly come into her life. He had lied to the elven army's general, leading him to the heart of Flykra, ironically during *Grato Amizade*. The small city was aglow with blue and white lights, a seven-moon celebratory event between the kingdoms of Erebus and Alun. Ulfred managed to convince the elves who had barged into his dwelling that this was where Ornella and Sayah were, enjoying the local festivities. I had warned my crew of the fleet ships on the shoreline just before, but without Ulfred, they would have found us right away. And I can only imagine the look of distress across the many families and friends gathered at the square, witnessing the untimely arrival of the elven army.

I was unsure what had become of Ulfred, but the day we arrived at his cottage's door, he had warned me not to use the *Ligação Mágica* to reach out to him. The land's magic was too dangerous with how many are hunting the *Marked Ones*. The green and gold swirls had revealed *Mae's* plan to flee Alizeh and return to Ulfred for sanctuary. The elders were spying on her every move before the twins' rite of passage. The very magic meant to be of convenience to us was being used to spy on our memories and thoughts.

We could no longer communicate using the magic; the risk outweighed the reward.

"Tell me what I have missed." She squinted at me before taking in the entire room, with its plain white walls, the only color being the brown dresser in the corner and the green curtains framing the small window adjacent to her bed. "Tell me, no matter how horrid. I must know."

Another few beats passed before I fell to my knees. I could see it there, the understanding in her eyes. She already knew, yet she was feigning ignorance because she wanted to hear the truth from me—that Ornella was gone.

A hot flush traveled up my chest and skin, my teeth clenching in response. Sayah's bewildered stare sent my heart clamoring recklessly, and I found myself reaching for her delicate fingers, intertwining them with mine.

Orbs of light flashed on my skin, traveling up and down my inky black swirls with a sense of urgency.

"I'm sorry."

The words were but a whisper, there and gone. Her throat bobbed as she shifted uncomfortably in the off-white sheets. Red lined the very windows to her soul, pupils dilating as she retracted her hand from mine, her chest rising and falling sporadically. "I wanted more than anything for you to wake up and find that your sister was waiting beside you," I pleaded, my voice uneven.

I awkwardly stood, perched at the edge of the bed, facing the window.

"I can't save her or the other *Marked Ones* without you; I need your connection to Ornella to help lead the way through Mount Auberon's caverns. Your power to drain energy is vital to our success."

And I held my tongue as a thought tickled at the soft spot in my mental fortitude that only she could pierce.

The truth is, I couldn't leave for the kingdom of Adara until you woke up.

I stared at my hands as they faced me, palms up, the silence in the room suffocating. With each passing moment, my panic began to spread.

It was cruel to think such a thought when I knew Tabitha needed me. She was why I started frantically searching the five kingdoms for a cure to the *Thereon*—my sole purpose for defeating their *Breeders*. Or so I had thought.

I could sense Sayah's stare on my back as I observed the green and gold magic from the room's sole window, peeking out from behind the curtains. The last of the day's sun trickled into the room, casting about an orange glow along the bland white walls.

"You do not need to be sorry, Nox." Her voice was gentle, soft. The tenderness of it had me looking in her direction, my vision hazy. Her hand reached for mine, and I was instantly at her side, taking in every detail.

Her lip quivered, and her delicate fingers squeezed my hand. "I am awake now and more than ready. It is time to rescue all *Marked Ones* and put an end to Bakunax's reign."

And the fire that abruptly flared inside her stormy eyes convinced me that we would.

Chapter Ten
Sayah

Nudging the door open, I peered through the crack, glancing down the hallway. The smell of lavender was replaced with something savory, wafting in from the direction of the kitchen. My stomach grumbled in response, and I immediately thought of Enid. She was a fantastic chef, and her meals were so distinct that my nose recognized her cooking. I smiled to myself, thinking of her completely at ease in the galley on the vessel where we first were acquainted. She had become Ornella's mentor and dear friend, and I could not think of her without thinking of my sister, too. I eased the door open, praying to the vine that it wouldn't creak.

Nox recently left at the request of unknown house guests, and my chest tightened in the newfound quiet, my hands shaking.

I did not want to be left alone.

The bland white walls felt suffocating; the room was too small. My first thought was to escape out the window to freedom, but as I stuck my head out of the opening, I discovered I was on the second story of the manor. The siding would be too precarious to climb down, and I could not risk injuring myself any further. As if on cue, a dull ache radiated from my abdomen as I leaned against the wall for support.

My muscles were stiff from neglect as my wounds took their time to heal. All the hard work I had put in on the ship, exercising and building my strength with Nox, felt as if it were all for nothing as I lay here unmoving in my deep sleep. The agonizing push-ups, sit-ups, and strenuous workouts... I huffed, crossing my arms as I bit the inside of my cheek, anger flushing my skin. I ruined my progress and would have to start from scratch. This is how it felt anyway.

I planned to have Enid explain the details of what had transpired. Sighing, I combed my fingers through my hair, fighting through the knots that had formed in my slumber as I sifted down the narrow walkway.

As I turned the corner to head in the direction of the kitchen, I heard a sound that stopped me in my tracks.

A soft melody originated from a room at the end of the corridor. I immediately pursued it, my eyes growing wide as I recognized the tune. The song was one *Mãe* would often play from her grand piano back in the Woodlands. I pictured her clear as day, her violet eyes closed as her fingers danced up and down the keys. The small studio would swell with the sound, resonating deep within my core. After she finished playing,

Mãe would always let the music taper off until we were met with silence. Only then would she gaze at me, smiling.

I flexed my fingers at my sides, and in that moment, I longed for a piano to play.

The door to the room was already cracked, and I nudged it open to meet the owner of the singing.

"Hello?" I called out, and the room went quiet. The space was nearly identical to mine, except the bed was next to the window. A woman lay tucked tight under the covers, from her chest down. Against my better judgment, I entered the room without permission, tiptoeing up to her cot.

Her brown hair was greying, and the skin that clung to her frail figure was as white as the sheets she lay beneath.

The expression etched across her features was haunting, my body freezing in mid-movement. All color had drained from her chapped lips; agony contorted her stiff face. If it were not for the fact that her chest rose and fell with steady breaths, I would have been certain that she was a ghost.

Her aura was all but a whisper around her, fading in and out of sight.

"Can you hear me?" I fumbled the words, pressing my middle and index finger on her neck to check for a pulse. It was strong and easy to find, its steady rhythm against my fingertips putting me at ease.

The air in the cramped space was stagnant, littered with dust particles.

"I'm going to open the window, if that's alright with you."

She didn't respond, her breathing slow and steady. I fought the window frame open, and it groaned in protest as I struggled, gasping at the exertion. My wound objected, pain pulling at my side.

"I did not think one could work up a sweat from opening a window, yet here we are." Wiping the sweat from my upper lip and hairline, I perched myself on the edge of her mattress while holding my tender abdomen.

Time passed as I stared out the window, the brisk night air flooding into the room and ruffling the strange woman's hair and sheets. I waited for the pain to subside, the dull ache a harsh reminder that I was awake and alive. The moon illuminated the endless fields of crops inside the vineyard, the plump fruit ripe and swollen, ready to be harvested. The glittering green and gold swirls of magic weaved through the landscape like a river, constantly flowing in the serene nature.

Ornella should've been in my stead, tending to the fragile woman. My sister would have cradled her inside a cocoon of energy, her gift nursing to what the stranger needed most. There was nothing I could do to help her heal, and my presence threatened to drain what energy she had left if I lost control. If the elders were here, they wouldn't have let me set foot in this room, let alone near anyone with an ailment.

My stomach growled, loud enough to distract me from my unease.

"Sorry, I haven't had a meal in a while," I muttered. She sighed in her wakeless state and shivered. She looked as though she hadn't enjoyed a meal in many lunations. My body was stiff as I fumbled to the window, pulling the frame closed as the wood cried out again. I half expected her to wake at this, and my heart jumped when I twisted around to face the unfamiliar figure.

But she was unmoving. The only sign of life was the rise and fall of her chest and beating heart that lay within, and her fading aura.

Her skin was soft as I stroked her cheek with my index finger, tucking her withered frame into the sheets. She was roughly the same age *Mãe* had been; her skin appeared made of porcelain, illuminated in the dim light.

I had an inkling that her soul was yearning for something. There were laugh lines in the creases of her eyes, at the corners of her mouth. There was a time when she enjoyed life and was surrounded by loved ones. *Where were they now?*

"I'll come back to visit you. Every day that I am here."

I carefully lifted her head slightly off the pillow, just enough to move her hair to one side. It was as I thought; her locks were matted and littered with knots.

My meal could wait.

I gently brushed through her brunette waves, my eyes beginning to water. There was a mirror on the far wall, its frame metallic gold. Staring into the reflection, I thought of *Mãe* adorning my crown with night water lilies.

The melody of my childhood began to drift through the space as I hummed for the woman the same song *Mãe* had last performed on the piano before she died.

Chapter Eleven

Sayah

I stood on the outskirts of the arena, staring at a group of primarily men wrestling each other to the ground. They were shirtless, not because of the heat radiating from the soil, but to show off the tribal markings they had earned from previous challenges against the other three clans. What I had learned in my time here was that the type of strength valued in the kingdom of Alun was the physical kind, and it was flaunted effortlessly by most. Typically, werewolves try to stay clear of challenging another pack member, but it happens once every blue moon. Their inky swirls, worn as badges of honor, were more than a sense of pride—it defined their worth inside a hierarchy that valued strength above all else.

This was information I gathered by listening to Odette gossip while she perched herself on my bed and ate breakfast with me every morning.

I still cringed at their natural confidence, pulling at the hem of my tunic to avoid biting my nails. The *Ligação Mágica* danced around them, following the grooves of the rolling hills. It was as if the land's magic was playfully observing, wanting to join in on the fun.

Soon, I would be joining the werewolves in their vigorous training. My injuries had begun to heal, and throughout one lunation, I had studied the clan's fighting techniques from afar. Time was slipping away from us, and each passing moment was a reminder of Ornella's confinement. And I felt mentally ready, at least to try and gain back the flexibility and stealth I had worked for on the ship with Nox. He told me it would be quite literally a matter of muscle memory, and I would recover what I had lost rapidly.

I'm almost positive he only said this to make me feel better.

Out of habit, I brushed the tips of my fingers over the tender area, which resulted in a dull ache, not the usual throbbing pain. It was progress. The involuntary wince sent a flutter of emotions throughout my chest, forming a lump in my throat.

It did not matter if my body was not yet fully healed; while I was out enjoying the daylight, my sister was a prisoner inside a dark, dreary cavern.

Her freedom was my responsibility.

A long breath escaped my lips, and to keep my eyes from watering, I tilted my face upward, eyelids closed.

The warmth of the sun slightly burned my skin, as I was still not used to its glaring exposure. An image of the kingdom's far-off mountains sprouted clearly in my mind's eye, their peaks cresting the low, ominous clouds. That was near Enid and Brom's home, where the ogres resided peacefully alongside the giants. *Well, before the Thereon attacked several of their camps looking for Marked Ones.* Alun's landscape did indeed rival Alizeh's; the luscious green grasslands were a breath of fresh air compared to the dense forestry. Nox's family had a long-standing vineyard that had managed to thrive for many lunations since the fall of the monarchies from long ago within the five kingdoms of Aksel. And he was next in line to inherit such a beautiful piece of history.

The sound of skin meeting its mark brought me back to the present. Two opponents had stepped out of line and were no longer sparring; from the look in their eyes, they had taken the fight personally. Their cordial match turned into a blood brawl, claws and fangs extracted as they howled in the momentary pause. I witnessed the warriors in training move with lethal precision, striking at one another until their claws made contact. The tearing of flesh gave me flashbacks to the day of my rite, when the *Thereon* attacked the helpless families on the ceremony grounds. Visions of my neighbors' faces wide with terror blurred my sight before I took my head in my hands. Blood splatter landed at my feet, tainting the green grass, and I staggered back.

Get it together, Sayah. I bit my lip, trying to force myself into the present and calm my labored breathing. *Bless the vine, my hands are shaking.*

I scanned the small crowd of bystanders near me, looking for a familiar face. A pair of dipped-in-honey orbs met mine, full of disdain. The young woman, whom I learned through word of mouth was Nox's soon-to-be mate, was staring daggers at me. Caelan was dressed in all black fighting gear, sweat dripping down her chin, arms crossed at her chest. The waves of light around her aura were bright, reminding me of Nox. Her spirit was strong, and I did not doubt that she was a natural-born leader.

I bit the inside of my cheek and pinched the bridge of my nose. *Why did she have to be here, of all beings?* There was only one way to fight off the flashbacks, and the power twisting inside of my core, desperate to be released.

Use logic, as Obsydora suggests, and don't go by feeling alone. Examine what is happening right in front of you.

I am here, in the kingdom of Alun, and no one is in danger.

There is no Thereon, and I will not hurt anyone.

I will not use my powers.

"Why the frown?"

Bless the vine, finally, someone I can trust. I jerked my head away from the sparring, my cheeks flushed. I flexed my fingers, my power trickling back into my core as the ogre's presence was immediately calming. Brom was standing there, looking out of place and dressed in formal attire. His trousers were more like a pair of capris, and the buttons on his collared shirt looked as though they would pop off at the simple flex of his chest muscles. He looked absolutely ridiculous. It took everything in me not to burst out into a fit of giggles.

"Why the strange outfit?" I retorted, raising a brow. "This is most definitely not your usual style. But it does, however, tickle my fancy." I wiggled my brows, pleased with the grin that spread across his features.

"I won't be sparring with the rest of you, unfortunately," he sighed, his vision skimming over the horizon to the east. "I'm to head with the chief as an elected peacemaker of sorts as he converses with the other three clans over the current...situation." At the last remark, he ran his fingers through his cropped brown hair, clearly exasperated.

All four clans are gathering for a meeting. This is unusual, as it is not a holiday or a full moon.

Nox's clan was the strongest of the four, the Fangs of the Fallen. He was to be mated to Caelan, the daughter of Chief Bjorn, the leader of the Iron Nightwalkers. I had yet to meet any members of the Bloodmoon Shadows or Crimsonclaw Howlers. Something was amiss for them to be meeting this suddenly, and an uneasy feeling crawled up my spine.

My focus shifted back to my friend, and I knew why they had picked Brom as the mediator; his chipper attitude and calm demeanor were the perfect contrast to the hot-headed chiefs who could ruin an entire kingdom's reign of peace with a single discussion. And ogres derived from Alun, so he naturally knew the terrain.

The lines on my forehead creased further, and I avoided his gaze by twisting back to the training ring.

"Where's Enid?" I asked to change the subject.

"Where do you think?" Brom laughed, his baritone echo traveling across the fields. "She's in the kitchen. You should go and see her." His voice turned soft, somber. "I haven't seen her this heartbroken since we lost our family. Her bond with Ornella is something else. When we first lost our kindred to the *Thereon,* I didn't think she'd open herself up to anyone again."

I bit my lip, fighting back the sudden urge to cry.

"But then you two showed up quite unexpectedly and joined our motley crew. And Ornella chose Enid, and moved her heart in ways that I can only comprehend as fate. Please go and see her, she needs a friend. She doesn't want to listen to advice from her brother." Brom chuckled and scratched his chin.

Did Ornella choose Enid?

I thought of their first encounter, how my sister desperately wanted to learn the basics of cooking. Her brazenness had taken Enid aback; how she bowed in respect to the ogress. Maybe they had both needed each other in more ways than just an extra pair of hands in the kitchen. I shook my head, deep in thought.

No, it was not simply Ornella choosing Enid. Their tendrils of light had picked each other out of understanding. Both women had lost their families, their homes. They had nothing in common, were different species with personalities that did not mesh. But through hardships, they formed a bond that most would search for in their entire lifetime.

"I'll go and see her tonight, after I spend time with Obsydora."

He nodded, satisfied with my answer.

We enjoyed each other's company in silence, watching the men and women spar against each other in the arena. The bystanders fidgeted next to me, their discomfort with my presence bordering on annoyance. I had always been hyperaware of what others were feeling, because I had been too concerned with how I affected others. Only recently had I started to try to ignore the sharp stares from those heading out into the fields, walking by with their chins held high. I could feel the disgust stemming from their core, teeth bared. The species here did not bother to hide their disdain for my mere existence; their beliefs that I was nothing more than an abomination were quite clear.

What would Mãe say if she were here with me? Would she try to shield me from their unfiltered opinions?

"I won't apologize for existing," I whispered to no one in particular. If Brom had heard me, he did not make it known. I swallowed, my throat dry. "I am starting my training with Obsydora today. *Do not* tell Nox." I started to chew on my nails, glancing at the ogre. Out of the corner of my eye, I witnessed Brom begin to fidget in place.

"Your wounds have only just healed, Sayah." He reached for me before pulling his hand back in hesitation. "There is no way that you are ready."

"Baby steps, Brom. I'll be starting small." I rubbed the back of my arms in anticipation, lightly jogging in place. "I can't wait forever. We don't have that kind of time."

Brom frowned, crossing his arms. He stayed silent, which meant that he disagreed, but I was right. Time was not on our side.

The hair on the back of my neck stood straight as an abrupt shout, followed by a thud, emanated from the training grounds. Both our heads snapped in its direction, and my heart nearly leaped out of my chest at the sight of Nox standing there with a man at his feet. He had flipped his opponent onto his back in one fell swoop, causing the man to scream, unwilling to accept defeat. The stranger lay on his back, hands behind his head.

My heart began to race inside my chest as Nox's stare intensified. Sweat lined his forehead, and I watched his exaggerated breaths as his chest rose and fell. All eyes were on the chief's son while his attention was affixed to me.

"Why are you out here?" Nox rumbled, fangs protruding from his mouth.

"What, am I not allowed to watch? The view is breathtaking." I gestured to the groups of men before me, a sly smile spreading across my features.

Nox's stare intensified, and it suddenly wasn't easy to breathe as I watched wide-eyed as he made his way over to Brom and me.

"Well, now you've done it." Brom laughed, rubbing his temples. "You know exactly how to get under his skin."

"I can't help it, he's easy to tease." I laughed, wiggling my eyebrows at the ogre.

It was true. I loved to tease Nox. This was most likely because I had zero idea of how to flirt with him, so I stuck to what I knew, which consisted of me failing to be mysterious and alluring, along with telling jokes.

He was then before me, the wind from his quick movements disheveling my hair. I could faintly hear Brom chuckle over the pounding of my heart in my ears. Nox took his callused hand and gently lifted my chin, forcing my attention to his beautiful sunset eyes.

"Only me." He leaned forward, his breath tickling my ear. "Only watch me."

Bless the vine. This brazen man made coherent thinking impossible, and I could not quiet the loud rhythmic beating in my chest. And I *knew* he could hear the fireworks of my heart plain as day.

I pulled away, narrowing my eyes at his mischievous grin.

"I'll start paying you attention when you give me something to watch." I stuck my tongue out at him and laughed as he raised his brows in shock.

"Don't tempt me, Sayah." There was a warning in his playful tone. "Or I'll show you why I'm next in line to be chief—right here, *right now.*"

My eyes dropped to his chest against my will, unable to keep my eyes off his defined muscles. Nox's body was covered in ink, the black swirls covering his abdomen, chest, and limbs. Sweat was dripping from his brow, and a low growl emitted from deep within his chest as he smirked.

He could have any of the women in his pack, and yet his gaze was fully consumed with me.

"I already have plans with someone else." I scoffed, pretending to wave him away. I peeked through one eye to see if he had left, and he was still standing in the same spot, but his smile was gone. He hadn't moved an inch.

"With whom?"

"A fickle dragon, who will burn me to a crisp if I am late."

Brom laughed, and I nearly jumped at the sound. I had forgotten that he was there and that we were in the middle of the fields just outside the vineyard. I glanced around the crowd and found Caelan staring at us, picking apart every interaction. She must hate me. I was thankful, in that moment, that Odette had revealed much of their family's secrets with delight as she scarfed down several crumpets with her morning tea.

Nox's mate had been arranged with the neighboring clan, the Iron Nightwalkers. She looked just how Odette described—a brazen warrior, more than qualified to be next to the men beside her. The left side of her head was shaved, and black swirls adorned her skull. What was left of her ash blonde waves cascaded past her shoulders and down her spine. Her eyes were almond-shaped, and in that instant, my imagination betrayed me, and I could see Caelan and Nox being the perfect leaders and uniting their clans.

Bless the vine, why did I torture myself with these thoughts?

Only after tasting blood from biting down on the inside of my cheek did I snap out of my self-wallowing.

"See you two at supper." I blew them both a kiss, smiling to myself as I turned in the direction of the sea.

"Do you want me to walk with you?" Nox called out from behind.

"You can walk with me next time. I want to be alone with my thoughts today."

I didn't turn to look at them as I headed to the main dirt road, afraid that if I met his gaze, he would come along anyway. Nox was used to me visiting my blue-scaled friend by the ocean, but today was different. Obsydora and I were working on something far more dangerous than physical strength.

I was training to defend myself against spiritual warfare.

The Sapphire dragon lay stretched across the meadow, the cool breeze carrying the faint smell of salt from the nearby ocean, rustling the tall grass around her figure. She reminded me of a porcelain figurine from a distance, the sun reflecting off her iridescent scales.

"I do not believe I have ever witnessed you so relaxed." My voice broke through the serene nature, staining the illusion of peace.

"You have never witnessed me away from the hatchlings, then." Obsydora hissed, displeased with my presence. "You're here early."

"This is the only form of training that I can do at the moment," I quipped, sitting cross-legged inches from her massive frame.

It was also the only excuse I could conjure to leave the manor and stroll quietly up the dirt road.

My reality sat heavily on my shoulders, its weight suffocating.

From the instant my eyes fluttered open, I had longed for a moment to grieve alone. The remnants of what was left of tears dried on my cheeks, and I wiped at them, cognizant that Obsydora might notice.

She blew a puff of smoke, the rings pushed by the wind before dissipating entirely. Her throat clicked as she grumbled something in dragon dialect, lifted her massive head off the grass, and craned her neck in my direction.

"What troubles you, *Marked One*?"

Bless the vine, she had noticed.

"The usual," I sighed, changing positions and pulling my knees to my chest. "So much time has passed...and I've accomplished nothing. I do not have the luxury of idly waiting and wasting my time watching shirtless men fight in a battle of egos. And I'm tired of being a nuisance to others." The long-winded confession sputtered from my lips, a flush of red burning the tips of my ears and neck.

A loud snort broke the few seconds of silence, followed by Obsydora standing and stretching her wings. They hovered above me, creating a shadow before tucking them in tight. She circled my figure, and I got the feeling she was sizing me up for some reason.

"You do not speak or act like a *Marked One* should," she retorted, and if dragons were able to frown, I was quite positive that was what she would be displaying in that instant—a look of disappointment. "You have rare powers that most of these ungrateful creatures roaming the five kingdoms would die for. It's time you start acting like it."

I bit my lip to keep myself from rolling my eyes. She knew nothing about me or what I had been through. Of course, I would always be grateful that she and the others from her horde flew us off the Isles of Cadogan, but she did not understand the scrutiny I had endured since my creation.

"How should I speak? How should I act?" I stood, finally meeting the eyes of one of the most revered creatures to have ever existed. They were reptilian in nature, though the luminescent hue of her golden irises held a playfulness that matched her feline personality.

"Proud, resilient." Obsydora crouched, ready to pounce.

The air caught in my throat, and I stumbled backward, catching myself with my palms, fingers intertwining with the thick, feathery grass.

She barked a laugh, easily jumping the distance between us, and her massive head hovered but inches away from mine. The dragon was motionless, the breeze catching several strands of my hair as they tickled my neck and skin. I was highly aware of every movement, of the tendrils of light that flickered wildly around her massive aura.

"Teach me," I pleaded, not bothering to hide my desperation. "Mold me into a being that can master her powers and protect those she cares for."

Obsydora stopped breathing. She tilted her head, but not before flashing her fangs and protracting her claws in a show of dominance.

"A soul cannot be shaped by another; only you have the ability to mold yourself into something new." She leaned forward, and her voice, shaped from brimstone and fire, was a gentle murmur that blended into the sounds of nature. "But I can show you the way."

And with that, her *Gavinhas* connected to mine, and the encompassing world was flooded by a bright light.

Chapter Twelve

Sayah

The white light obscuring my vision slowly began to dissipate until I found myself inside a familiar forest, and Obsydora was nowhere to be seen.

"Hello?" I called out into the vacant woodlands resembling Alizeh's in the winter. A soft layer of snow covered the pine branches and soil, though not nearly as beautiful as Erebus's iridescent white landscape. As I stepped forward, my head turned in all directions in search of my dragon companion.

Obsydora didn't camouflage herself, did she?

I groaned, my shoulders sagging. Whatever game she was playing reminded me of Kazumi's usual chaos. That pesky little fairy was undoubtedly up to no good and might be in cahoots with Obsydora. *Bless the vine and all things sacred*; if those two were conspiring together, I was in trouble.

"You can come out now—enough of the childish games," I taunted, which was a blatant lie because I, in fact, loved games. What I did not love was being spooked by some of the scariest creatures known to exist in the five kingdoms. At that moment, I could envision Kazumi's razor-sharp teeth and her evil grin as she once again sent me reeling from her ridiculous teasing.

The sound of my boot snapping a twig beneath my feet sent a shiver of fear down my spine, pulling me out of my spiraling thoughts.

Get it together, Sayah. This is precisely why Obsydora put you in this predicament in the first place.

My focus shifted to the *Ligação Mágica*. The land's magic was full of life. The green and gold swirls traveled up the tree trunks, snaking their way through the natural landscape. It seemed sentient, aware of my presence as I began walking forward, responding to my touch.

This was odd; the magic's reaction reminded me of the shifting of seasons, when the thin veil between us no longer existed. Wait; that was it! The Ligação Mágica was the answer! I grinned, splaying my fingers into the iridescent swirls before snapping my fingers in victory.

"*Liguero*." No sooner than the words escaped my lips, I was racing through the wintry mix, scanning my surroundings for any hint of an aura or their *Gavinhas*.

But there was nothing, not a hint of life could be found scampering across the cold, dry twigs and crumpled leaves littering the forest floor. Not a single rabbit, squirrel, or any of the woodland animals made their way out of the burrows. I scanned the ground, seeing the untouched webs and settled dirt, without so much as a single trail of pawprints—proof of the living. And in a crippling realization, I ran my fingers through my hair, my heart beginning to race.

I was alone, a fate worse than death.

"Please, answer me!" I screamed, tears forming as I ran, my feet losing traction on the wet earth. The ground beneath me felt all too real, and this was not a memory, but some version of the present. I was now kingdoms away from my friends and the horde of dragons. A lump formed in my throat, and haggard breaths escaped my lungs. "This joke has gone on for far too long, Obsydora. Show me how this is helping me gain control of my gift; I am failing to see the point here." Anger laced my pleading tone, my lip quivering when I was met with silence once more.

A low hum then shook the earth, growing in intensity. My palms pressed against the soil, the green and gold swirls anchoring me to the forest floor. I was making no progress with my current approach to the situation. Another flashback of the day of my ceremony crossed my thoughts, of me falling to the ground in desperation to find *Mãe* after the *Thereon* had attacked the ceremony grounds. I had been desperate to see her, and it was only when I reached out to the *Ligação Mágica* that I found her.

Casting spells was never the answer, as *Mãe* had taught Ornella and me growing up. A twinge of guilt surged through me as I thought of my sister, unable to free herself from her prison. And I could picture her there, strong even in the presence of the *Thereon* and their wicked *Breeders.*

I must stay strong, if not for me, for her. She's depending on me.

Ornella had been my shield from all life's woes, the one who had protected me from the beginning, taking the brunt of all the hardships we endured.

Were we fated to be Marked Ones, or had the Creator cursed us from the beginning?

The unknown was indeed a burden, but so was the blaring truth. And it was because of this that I needed to do everything possible to repay my debt. My breathing slowed, and my body shook as I fought the urge to let my powers siphon the plants and energy encircling me. Still, no birds chirped, and no crickets hummed their gentle songs as I succumbed to nature. Time itself must have stopped as I squeezed my eyes shut, giving in to the stillness.

"Show me." My voice was but a muted whisper. I was no longer entirely sure who I was speaking to, whether it was Obsydora, my inner self, or someone else entirely.

And then I felt it—a pull on my *Gavinhas.*

It was slow, at first. My soul trickled into the magic, the tendrils of light lurching into the unknown as my consciousness weaved its way across the embedded soil. The cool touch of the plants brushed against me, releasing a tingle of tranquility that seeped into my core. Mother Nature's tender kiss on my soul resembled how flowers bloom beneath the sun, the warmth dissipating my unease.

I snaked through the forest until I found myself before a familiar scenery, and an eerie figure. The woman stood at the base of the *Videira,* seemingly lost in thought. Her gaze was fixated on the vine; palms pressed against the translucent green trunk. Orbs of light swirled inside the sentient being from her touch. The massive plant stretched far across Alizeh, and yet all the magic and light that traveled through its greenery converged on a singular spot. Clouds of color absorbed into one another, dancing at her slender fingertips. All I could perceive was the back of her head, the woman's raven hair cascading past her waist.

She leaned forward and kissed the *Videira*, but not before speaking, her unintelligible words gentle yet full of sorrow.

"Hello?" I called to her, taking a step in the stranger's direction.

The sound of a twig snapping from behind us broke through the ominous wood, and the stranger's head spun around, leaving my mouth agape.

The being before me was none other than *me*, with eyes as black as night and a look of terror etched across her familiar features. Her hands never left the vine, and her arms shook as she fought to hold her composure.

"I can no longer ignore the evil that has seeped into their hearts." Her lip quivered at her admission, tears staining her chapped cheeks. She turned her head in the direction of the sound of a twig snapping nearby. "This is the only way."

A rush of heat spread up my neck and ears as I stumbled at the reverence in her tone. There was something too familiar about this scene, the suffocating feeling that the demise of this woman, *who resembled me*, was impending. She may bear a resemblance to me in features, but I knew we were not the same. Wisdom radiated from her tendrils of light—and though her *Gavinhas* were onyx like mine, they illuminated like Obsydora's.

Her soul was thousands of lunations old.

A sudden tug on my tendrils of light pulled me back into the *Ligação Mágica*, where the green and gold swirls of magic filtered me into a field of warmth and bright light. It was no longer winter; the goosebumps that had trailed my skin vanished instantaneously.

The sapphire dragon sat on the waves of soft grass, and her yellow eyes glimmered with a deep emotion.

"*What was that?*" I threw my arms up in the air, spinning in a circle. I breathed a sigh of relief, seeing the rolling hills and vineyard nearby. "You said you would help me train, not scare the never-ending daylights out of me."

Perplexed, I lifted a brow. "Did Kazumi put you up to this by chance?"

Her tail flicked like a cat's, mouth slightly parted, displaying her canines. There was a silence that followed. I frowned, fighting to tap my foot just like *Mãe* used to when she wanted an answer from Ornella or me. Obsydora let out a puff of smoke and tilted her head upward, eyes closed as she basked beneath the sun's rays.

"That was not my doing, *Marked One*." She answered after I went and sat beside her, using her as a shield from the warm wind blowing in from the sea. It smelled of salt and earth, mixed with the scent of freshly blooming peonies. The sun was beginning to set, the stars already overtaking the pink and orange hues in the sky.

I glanced down at my hands in my lap, and they shook, the adrenaline from whatever I had witnessed earlier still coursing through me. The power within me simmered to life, churning with my unease.

"Why won't you call me by my name?" I whispered, fighting back a sudden surge of tears. There was no reason to cry, yet I was overwhelmed with emotion. Perhaps it was the build-up of everything, the pressure I felt to be as close to perfect as possible.

"You have not given me a reason to." The fickle dragon was up on her feet, nudging me with the end of her nose, urging me to stand. She positioned herself further back, at the opposite end of the field. "Prove yourself worthy of a dragon, *Marked One*. And I will speak your name into existence."

The doors swung behind me as I entered the manor, the immediate change in temperature warming my cheeks. It was past supper, and I had stayed out far longer than anticipated, sitting in Obsydora's company to calm my nerves. A savory smell filled my nostrils, and my stomach growled.

"I bet Enid let Brom eat any leftovers," I sighed, my shoulders sinking as I trudged through the entryway and over to the side of the house, where I rarely set foot.

The kitchen was empty, except for a glowing light in the far corner and the strong remnants of delicious food. I tiptoed into the unfamiliar space, feeling out of my element with the looming cutlery hanging from hooks above the three wooden stoves. The remaining embers glowed, illuminating the knives displayed on the countertop's clean surface.

One of the cabinet doors swung open urgently, revealing a head of auburn curls.

"Oh, it's just you," Odette quipped, ignoring me as she continued to rummage through the various drawers. I gasped, falling back onto the tile floor and landing hard on my buttocks.

"What are you doing?" I hissed while awkwardly standing. She was oblivious to my evident irritation, erratically searching the kitchen with an urgency.

"What does it look like? I'm trying to find something."

I pinched the bridge of my nose and deeply sighed. "That's obvious. *What* are you looking for? Maybe if you'd tell me, I could help you."

"Ahah!" A loud pop followed the sound of triumph, and I opened my eyes to Odette holding a cylindrical container with a mystery item inside. She licked her lips, ignoring me as I approached.

"*Fogoe.*" She uttered the spell before I could realize what she was doing. The snap of her fingers ignited the magic in the air, and the green and gold swirls outside the kitchen window reacted, dancing along the windowsill and momentarily flowing inside the room.

"Odette!" I whisper shouted her name in disbelief, then sprinted through the kitchen entryway to make sure no one else was around. "You shouldn't use magic! Who knows who could be watching?"

"No, *you* shouldn't use magic. You're the *Marked One*. I'm just an ordinary werewolf who wants her sweet treat warmed up. Is that so bad?" She shoves a handful of brown mush into her mouth. "No, no, it's not. Not at all." Several more fistfuls of the dessert are shoved into her mouth until she looks like a giant chipmunk with swollen cheeks.

I stare in disbelief and watch as she carelessly eats to her heart's content, sitting cross-legged on the kitchen floor. The smile that spread across my face was genuine, and I went to sit next to her in the candlelight.

"So, whose food are you eating?" I raised a brow, and she froze, her attention sliding over to me for the first time.

"Who says I'm stealing?"

"I would bet all my gold coins the dessert sitting in your lap is not yours." I made a point to gesture around the empty room. "You came after supper, when you knew nobody would be around. And if you weren't afraid of being caught, then why did you hide when I entered?"

She gulped while looking away, but continued to enjoy her findings.

"To tell you the truth, I used to eat my sister's leftovers and treats all the time," I said absentmindedly, staring into space. "I know you stole it, because I've done the same."

There was a pause, and a weighted intensity spread throughout the dim lighting.

"Mmmm," Odette considered, and she rubbed her chin, smearing chocolate on her face. "How would your sister react when she found out you ate her food? Because I'm almost certain that if Enid finds out I ate some of the dessert she made for tomorrow, she'll be upset."

"Some? You've eaten almost all of it!" The laugh I barked caught in my throat, and I glared at her dubiously. "Did you say Enid? *Bless the vine,* you foolish child. That ogress will eat you alive if she finds out!" I then leaned toward her, whispering, "Or worse, she'll make you wash the dishes by yourself after supper. You'd be in here until sunrise."

Odette rolled her eyes, placing a lid on the container. "You're starting to sound like an old lady. I thought you were cool." She jumped up suddenly, pointing a finger at me. "That's right! I nursed you back to health; you shouldn't be nagging me at all!"

"What are you two doing?"

We both froze in place, our eyes widening as a deep female voice emerged from the shadows of the hallway. Time stood still as Enid entered her domain, only to find Odette with her arms wrapped around the large bowl like a greedy troll, covered in chocolate, and me crouched on the floor, seemingly her accomplice.

"It was all her!" I pointed back at the young werewolf, who glared daggers in my direction.

"Oh, I have a bone to pick," She sauntered into the room, wagging a finger in the air. "But not with the girl. With you, Sayah." Her arms crossed, and Enid's glare was as sharp as her chef's knife.

"Me? I'm not the one who ate your food!"

"Ah, yes, my point exactly. You never eat my food. You're staying out till dusk, missing supper, and overexerting yourself when you should be resting."

The ogress's lip trembled, her soft brown eyes telling me what she struggled to say aloud. *How will we rescue Ornella with you acting this way?* A few strands of hair fell in front of her face, and the hand she had extended to me was now inside her trouser pocket.

"I'm sorry, Enid. I won't skip a meal again," I apologized, bowing my head.

It was deathly quiet for several beats until the sound of Odette shamelessly licking her fingers broke the silence.

"Good," Enid replied as she crossed her arms while sighing. "Let's get you two cleaned up; the girl especially. She looks as though she fell straight into the batter."

"What is it that you made?" I pondered, trying to catch a glimpse of the large bowl.

"It is a sugary dough, with pieces of chocolate mixed into the batter. You break it apart and roll it into small balls, and place them on a metal sheet before sliding them into the oven to bake. They are called chocolate chip cookies.

"Would you like to try some?" She then briefly studied Odette, shaking her head in disapproval. "Not you, you've had enough. I'm surprised you do not have a tummy ache."

Enid swooped in, grabbing the bowl from Odette and placing it on the countertop. She made her way around the kitchen with ease, holding utensils and items from the various cabinets as I sat on the floor, observing. The ogress practically breathed the fire into the oven, her movements swift and concise. I wondered if my sister would ever get to her level of comfort in the kitchen, knowing how awkward she was. We all three sat on the tile floor, staring at the single lit candle, the burning wax seeping into its base.

"Ornella would love chocolate chip cookies," I whispered into the night, pulling my knees close to my chest. Enid hummed in agreement beside me as she gently nudged my shoulder.

"She's finding her way in the kitchen. She's improving."

"Really?" I turned to face her fully, and the disbelief on my face must have been evident because she shook with laughter.

"Yes, really. Ornella needed someone who would be patient with her. You do not learn how to cook a roast on your first day." Enid rose back to her feet, dusting off her clothes. "They're ready."

Odette and I stared in awe with our hands extended, ready to receive the delicious treat. A dessert of this stature was surely a gift from the heavens. The smell of freshly baked chocolate wafted in front of our noses, and I began to drool. It was then that my stomach grumbled, and I remembered that I had yet to eat supper.

I picked the cookie up off the plate, and it fell apart almost immediately.

"Hey!" I frowned, looking at the mush sitting on my plate.

My friend shook her head, amusement dancing across her features. "Eat it anyway, Sayah. Trust me."

The plate tipped forward as I shoveled the warm dough into my mouth. I gasped, holding a hand over my lips to keep the contents from falling to the floor. This dessert was better than delicious. It may be my new all-time favorite, trumping the infamous chocolate-filled croissant from the local bakers back inside my village in the Woodlands.

"This is...amazing."

Odette, who had been quiet for some time, burst into laughter. "You look as if you're in love with your food, Sayah."

A genuine grin spread across Enid's face, her eyes glowing bright in the candlelight. "That is the best compliment a chef can receive, girl. When you witness someone fall in love with your food, it is a memory that will sit with you for this life and the next."

"I'll make sure always to tell you just how much I enjoy your meals." I stared at her in earnest, placing my hand lightly on her forearm. "I promise to make it back in time for supper."

Odette swiped the rest of my cookie out of my hand, breaking the tension as she ran out the kitchen door in a fit of giggles. I could hear her call from the hallway, her voice fading, "I promise always to finish your food, if Brom doesn't first!"

Enid and I were alone for the first time since our arrival in Alun.

"Do you miss her?" I asked, the blush rising to the tips of my ears. They had been nearly inseparable from the instant they began working with each other on Nox's vessel. I knew Ornella held the ogress close to her heart and treasured their friendship.

"I miss her every day." Her eyes glimmered in the dim light, tears pulling at their corners. "Do your best to heal so that we can see her soon." The soft desperation in her voice caused a lump to form in my throat.

I hugged her, and her arm across my mouth muffled my declaration.

"I'll do my best."

Chapter Thirteen

Sayah

This was by far the most challenging task I had ever set out to accomplish. It was more difficult than the summer I first learned to keep up with *Mãe* on the piano.

I remembered those days clearly, when she would make me practice our duet for an upcoming recital nonstop, until the days would fade into night, and I would play until my soul blended into the song. She would tap her foot, her arms crossed, as she examined my posture and the way my fingers made contact with each key. It was the summer I had declared I would be the one to take over her music academy. *Mãe* was not going to make it easy;

she wanted me to earn that right. This had been the one passion in my life I was willing to fight for. My love for music transcended all the pain and hurt I had experienced from being treated as an outcast by my peers. It had been my goal for many lunations, but that dream was now but a blur in the back of my heart, obscured by life's painful indifference. It was a regret for what could have been.

With the future uncertain, I had but one goal: to unlearn everything I knew about my gift. For the next several moons, I fought to release the power from my core without emotions attached. This proved to be most intimidating; the gift pulsing underneath my skin in protest. I was close to asking Nox if I could train my combat skills with him over the grueling internal battle waging its silent war.

"Again."

Yes, I most definitely am in need of a break from this.

My shoulders sank, and I wiped the sweat from my brow using the back of my hand. I fought the urge to cry out in defeat, my emotions rippling across my face as I fought to bury them.

Obsydora hissed, her tongue flicking out of her mouth in warning. *Bless the vine, my poker face is horrendous.*

With my fingers splayed, palms facing the earth, I shut out the rest of the world, focusing on draining the energy of the dandelion placed at my feet, without syphoning the energy of the grass encompassing it.

To an outsider, the exercise would appear to be child's play.

But to hone the constant riptide of power, fighting to escape my fingertips at a moment's notice was, I dared to say, daunting.

Let it be second nature, the same as lifting your hand to your face, equal to your soul waking as the sun rises, and resting when the world is quiet and the moon looms overhead. Do not think of your power as the Creator's, but as an extension of you.

I mulled over Obsydora's advice as I brushed back the few strands of hair obscuring my vision. Earlier that day, Odette had braided my hair away from my face to help keep it out of the way during training. My raven mane now hung limp over my shoulder as I took a deep breath and attempted to view the world through a new lens.

Confirmed by Obsydora, all *Marked Ones* could see *Gavinhas*. I remembered how vivid the sky had become, the auras and tendrils of light emitting from each being that first time at the rite-of-passage ceremony. The day my powers had truly awakened, the reason why the *Videira* had responded to mine and my sister's touch.

I ground my teeth together at the memory. It was the day I had lost *Mãe*, the woman whom I loved most in all five kingdoms. She was no longer with us, because my sister and I had unknowingly let the *Thereon* know of our presence.

Many had been lost that day due to ignorance.

One could argue that it was the elder's fault, for not informing the elven army of the looming threat, not warning the entire village of what was coming, and the state of the kingdoms around us. The villagers had been too sheltered to know any better.

"You need the strength to siphon the energy from hundreds of *Thereon*." A growl ripped through my thoughts, catching me off guard. "Why are you holding yourself back?"

"Because I've already failed." I glanced at my feet, tears falling into the grass below. "Ornella and I cannot go back. She can't go back to the home she adores because of me." Heat spread along my cheeks and down my neck as I squeezed my eyes shut. "I'm afraid. And I'm scared. I can't fail again. And the *Thereon* have no obvious weakness. They're too strong."

Obsydora adjusted her feet in the grass, the sun blinding me momentarily as its light rippled across her sapphire scales.

"Your fear is not based in reality, *Marked One*. See them for what they are: animated corpses. The body usually knows it is dying before the soul does. In this case, the soul is long perished, but their limbs still move, their heart still drums in their hollow chest. The *Thereon* are an empty shell of what should have been; their fate whisked away so cruelly. It is a shame."

There it was again—the inconvenient whisper of guilt and empathy.

The very concept of a *Thereon* was heartbreaking. I did not want to end what was left of their life, because once I did, they would disappear. All that remained was a shadow of their past, melded by greed and tainted desire. They had once had loved ones, dreams, and aspirations.

I did not want to erase the only sign that they had ever existed.

"Who they were vanished along with their *Gavinhas*. You must do this to save those who still have a chance. The living."

I opened my eyes, nodding.

My hands began to tingle as the black wisps of power extended past the length of my fingertips, brushing against the flower's petals, sweat dripping along my forehead. The aura encompassing the plant began to fade, the bright light dimming around my serpentine grip. Though it was a modest flower, I did not want to harm it. I concentrated all my efforts on not devouring the delicate form of life. Still, I could sense a change within my control as energy overflowed from my core, swelling inside me—it consumed every inch of space in my body, tugging on my negative emotions.

I glanced sideways at Obsydora, who observed from a distance, tail twitching. There was no indication that she would come to my rescue if things went awry, if I were to lose control. My gift could unleash havoc on the fields of nearby fresh crops, destroying the livelihoods of many families, including Nox's.

A small cry escaped my lips as I pictured the silent storm raging across the rolling hills, sweeping over the landscape as the grass wilted and faded to ash.

No, I wouldn't let that happen. I was not a monster, and I was determined to prove it one way or another. The muscles in my legs tensed in pain as my feet dug into the soil, firmly planting me. The *Ligação Mágica* swirled around me in haste, sensing the change as my veins began to bulge out of my skin.

The life of the dandelion evaporated as it fell limp, my abilities hungry, not yet satiated.

"Please, no," I whimpered, watching the earth transform from green to black as I siphoned the vibrancy from nature. "Why can't I do it? Why won't it listen to me?" My desperation reached the sapphire dragon as she approached with her head low, the grass tickling her chin.

"How much energy must I drain until I can master this simple skill? Will it take me draining all of life before I can control it?" A loud sob erupted from my chest, carrying another wave of power, breathing its curse into the land and spreading past the meadow and beyond. Flames abruptly tickled my skin, and I let out the breath I had been holding, crying out in pain. The black wisps recoiled into my figure, snaking their way into their vessel—me.

"What was that?" My scream echoed off into the distance. The smell of smoke met my nostrils, and I studied the hairs on my arms; they were singed from the fire. Obsydora breathed directly at me. I turned my heel and faced the dragon, crossing my arms. "Were you trying to scorch my skin and make me your next meal?"

"No," she snapped, her massive teeth barred in my direction. "I was keeping the crops safe from your lack of control." Her massive head dipped low, inches from my figure. "That is enough practice for today. Tomorrow we will try again elsewhere."

"Soon there won't be anywhere else for us to try," I grumbled, taking in the devastation I caused in a matter of seconds.

"Your negativity will be your ultimate downfall," she barked beside me.

Rolling my eyes, I began chewing on my thumbnail as I used my two remaining brain cells for the day to think. "Then, what do you suggest? Should I start to siphon energy with a smile on my face? Am I supposed to enjoy it?"

As soon as I said it, I knew I was in trouble. A blunt force hit me in the back of the head, sending me tumbling into a bed of thorns in the nearby brush. My hands stung as the spikes cut through my palms, which were now covered in blood.

Obsydora snarled, her anger sending shivers down my spine. Her tail swished back and forth, the culprit of my pounding headache. She reminded me yet again that she was a dragon, one of the most revered creatures in all five kingdoms, and that I, whatever my origins were, did not matter. I was not in charge. And I was a fool for being sarcastic and not showing respect.

I bowed my head, shame heating my cheeks.

"Do not use that nasty attitude with me. Your gift *is* a gift from none other than the *Creator*. It is intentional; you must be at peace with this knowledge."

"Why would they intentionally give me the ability to siphon energy?"

"Perhaps you should stop asking why and accept it."

A silence began to grow between us as I considered her words. A gentle breeze brushed across my cheeks; a sudden change in the wind's direction caused goosebumps to travel up my spine as a new thought gave birth amid my self-wallowing.

I could accept the gift; accept myself for the way I am.

The sun blazed overhead, and I shielded my eyes from its intensity. A lump formed in my throat as words failed me.

Am I allowed to like my gift? I mean, it is named a gift. I should like it, right?

Coming to terms with this part of me went against every fiber of my being. I had been taught to hide it, pretend it didn't exist, that I didn't exist. Knots of anxiety began to form at my shoulders at the mere idea of accepting the piece of me I hated. It was the reason I had been ostracized from my peers, the reason for all of my life's woes. I raised a brow as I examined my hands, turning them, palms facing up.

But I did enjoy the idea of going against the grain, against what the priests and elders wanted for me.

A sly grin spread across my features, and I rubbed the remaining tears out of my eyes. "I'll think about it," I whispered, and she chortled before blowing fumes across my path.

Obsydora stretched her wings, her scales the color of the ocean as they reflected the light. She was then airborne, creating a whirlwind of dirt and leaves that encompassed me. The fickle dragon gave me a nod and ascended into the clouds without so much as a parting goodbye.

I waited for the dust to settle before heading back to the estate.

The heavy weight on my chest felt a little lighter as I ambled along, content in silence, and unbeknownst to me, this was my first spark of peace.

Chapter Fourteen

Tabitha

Beneath me, the army of *Thereon* were preparing for war. Several of their *Breeders* had crawled out from the center of Mount Auberon. The putrid creatures melded from evil had slithered up from the depths of the abyss to join us. I never witnessed more than one or two at a time, but at least seven slumped to the floor below, hissing at the crowd of *Thereon* encircling each beast.

The soulless creatures were feeding on the *Breeders* and growing in strength. The black parasitic magic clung to their opaque skin, and the beings they once were, lost inside their deformed figures. If I squinted hard enough at their figures, the outlines of who they were previously could be detected. Ogres, trolls, dwarves, elves, all the species inside the five kingdoms had been turned with the blood of their maker. Just a drop of the vile liquid would penetrate straight into one's core and grasp at their *Gavinhas*, draining their tendrils of light. The *Thereon* were now just an extension of the one who controlled all that moved inside this mountain, the former dragon known as Bakunax.

I did not feel bad for them, not in the slightest. Forced to witness the monstrosities of the crimes committed by the *Thereon* to the *Marked Ones* in the cages hanging next to mine, their sins unforgivable. Who the *Thereon* once were had long left this earth. Black auras were all that surrounded the creatures; their souls withering into nothing.

Never to reincarnate.

"Tabitha!"

My focus left the foreboding scene on the cavern floor, and I turned to the young woman to the right of me, my hands still tightly gripping the metal bars. A vibrant blue magic encompassed each floating prison, threatening any being who ventured inside without permission, as well as those trapped inside venturing too far out. I remembered the moment when I had reached my arms out in desperation, only to be flung backwards by an electrifying pain. The elf had said her name was Ornella, and she had been captured in the kingdom of Erebus. That fact alone had surprised me, as elves did not leave their homelands. What she was doing in the kingdom, farthest from her usual habitat, had almost piqued my interest enough to ask.

I raised a brow, refusing to speak. If I answered her, there was a good chance the man who had captured me, that annoying brat, would appear from amongst the shadows. He was as conniving as he was wicked.

He would come periodically to make himself known, whispering sinister things in Ornella's ear. At first, I had begged her to tell me what he was up to. But her eyes would go wide with fear, her lip trembling as she shook her head no. The man was toying with her, a cat with a mouse in the palm of his hands.

She pressed her face against the rusted bars of her cage, and there was an urgency in her tone. "Tabitha, are there stairs leading directly to the cavern floor?"

I frowned, my shoulders slumping as I sighed, dragging my hand down my face. "If I said there was, what good would it do you?" My whisper on the urge of being too loud, I paused, catching myself. I gestured to the area around us, my patience waning. "Even if you managed to escape the cages—" I pointed to the strikingly blue ancient magic encompassing the dozens of captives, "—I doubt you could make it a few feet before you were turned into a *Thereon*, or eaten by their *Breeders*."

"No, you're wrong." Her tone was cross, and she began to pace the width of her prison. "If that were true, we would have been eaten already. We are too important to Bakunax and whatever he's devised. Our gifts have been deemed valuable; more so than his mounds of gold."

A growl ripped from my throat, and I shook my head. "*No, you're wrong, Ornella.*" I turned to my left, my eyes watering as I glanced at the several empty cages. "I thought the same as you. I have tried to think of every possible solution to escape, the same as you." Tears painted my cheeks, and I wiped my face in disbelief. I could still cry, even in this state of dehydration. "Others have tried and failed. And for their insolence, they were eaten."

A silence invaded the space, and I could feel her glare from behind. My nails dug into the palms of my hands as I fought for composure. She did not understand, not in the slightest. *I was her*, the same fool who dreamed of seeing the sun and feeling the warmth of its light on my skin. That same skin was now littered with dirt and bruises, my wrists sore from the shackles digging into my flesh.

"All hope is not lost."

My head snapped up at the statement, and I whipped around as if she had challenged me to a duel. I met her stare, ready to slice through any hope she had left. To my surprise, her emerald eyes held not only fear but courage, radiating from her soul.

"I have never been able to afford to lose hope, not when so many have depended on me since my creation." Ornella broke character, the lump in her throat visible as she swallowed. She squinted into the darkness, her body so still she could have been suspended in time. "Mine and Sayah's gifts are essential in this upcoming war. I know this because I have been talking with the man who murdered my *mãe*. I will make him divulge everything, even if that is what it costs me."

My mouth fell open, and I examined the elven woman with a newfound clarity.

"What has he told you?" I asked, leaning forward with anticipation.

She took a step back, putting a finger to her lips. Immediately, she dropped into a fetal position, facing away, and began humming a lullaby.

I slowly lowered myself to the cage's metal surface, sitting cross-legged on the floor. *Why had she stopped talking?* It was usually hard to get her to be quiet and stay still. But then I heard it; the sounds of feet echoing up the hidden staircase carved into the stone.

And he appeared, stepping out of the shadows and into the dim light. His multicolored eyes were transfixed on Ornella as he took each step with consideration, quietly approaching. His fixated glare grew in intensity, pupils dilated. The unappealing sight caused my skin to crawl. I did my best to make myself small, sinking back until I felt the prison's bars digging into my spine. The monster reached into her cage, my breath catching as he delicately massaged her white locks between his fingertips. He did not bother to filter his emotions. The man looked at her as if she were everything to him and nothing all at once.

Chapter Fifteen

Ornella

Staying strong for others was second nature to me—staying strong for myself, however, was a different story. I continued to hum the lullaby *Mãe* would sing to Sayah and me as children, ignoring the man who played with my hair through the cage bars.

It took everything in me not to lash out and exact revenge for his sins. He was the reason many elves lost their lives on the day of my ceremony; the reason *Mãe* was no longer with us.

I cleared my throat, flipping over to directly face my enemy. His hair was white like mine, a detail only noticeable if you were within inches of his face. The parasitic magic that clung to his skin was not as active today, the black web continuously moving along his skin. The gleam inside his green and gold eye quickened the pace of my heart, and I fought the urge to swat his hand away.

"Why have you come to visit me?" My voice was soft, and my eyes were wide with confusion. I hoped that I accurately portrayed myself as weak and innocent. I needed to gain his trust, and today my goal was to learn his name.

One would assume this would be a simple task, but this man made it nearly impossible to obtain information. So far, all I knew was that my sister and I were critical key factors in Bakunax's plan, and he was patiently waiting for Sayah to show up at his doorstep.

Sayah. My stomach flipped at the thought of her, a pain shooting through my chest. The last time I had seen her, the man in front of me had stabbed her in the side with his blade, her screams still haunting me every time I closed my eyes.

"No reason in particular," he murmured, holding out a piece of bread and an apple, which he stowed away in his robe pocket.

He's lying. I spun the apple in my hand, inspecting it before taking a bite.

"Thank you for the food." My eyes lowered to my lap, unable to look him in the eye as I thanked him.

His finger was suddenly under my chin, tilting my face to meet his gaze. "You are welcome." The corners of his mouth turned upward into a smile, and in that instant, he appeared venomous, a predator waiting for his chance to strike.

I ripped my face away from his, unable to hide my scowl. Laughter erupted from him, echoing into the caverns and bouncing off the walls.

"I was waiting to see how long your act would last this time." He stretched his arms, sighing. "I lied. There is something I want to know."

At this, I was alert, sitting on my knees with my hands resting in my lap. This was the opportunity I had been waiting for so desperately. I paused, waiting for him to speak, biting the inside of my cheek to keep my questions from escaping my lips.

He scratched his bare face, deep in thought. "What do you know about your powers?"

My lips tightened, and I watched as he licked his own and leaned away. It was a question within a question, and my knuckles turned white as I steadied my breathing. He sought information without revealing his true intentions or reasoning.

"A trade," I snapped, and took another bite of my apple. "I will answer your question if you answer one of mine."

I had more than a thousand questions to ask this man.

Why did he accuse Sayah and me of ruining his life? What does he gain from working with Bakunax? How did he manage not to get turned into a Thereon, and what is the magic he is encased in? Why are his Gavinhas silver, but he is not a Marked One? If he is not an elf, then what is he?

The wicked grin returned; his features were frightening in the cast of the shadows.

"Answer me first, and I will consider your request, depending on your question."

I clenched my jaw, averting my eyes over to Tabitha. She was paying us no attention, or doing a marvelous job pretending not to. If I had options, I would disagree to his terms. But it was painfully apparent that either I did what this man said, or I would suffer the consequences. He was not allowed to hurt me directly because he would often threaten Tabitha's safety if I did not comply.

"I give energy to the earth and those around me."

He groaned at my obvious answer, his eyes changing emotions in an instant, now narrowed at me like daggers.

"What else?" His voice dropped, irritation lacing his tone. I gulped, desperately peering into the cavern looking for the correct reply. He would refuse to listen to my question if I did not provide him with the answer he wanted.

"All *Marked Ones* can perceive auras, and one's *Gavinhas*. A being's soul." As I answered, a shiver ran down my spine. My jaw clenched as I witnessed an array of emotions briefly flicker across his face. I hated myself in that moment for being afraid of this man.

"Are those the only differences between ordinary beings and *Marked Ones*?" he asked, examining his nails.

The only difference? I chewed on the inside of my cheek as I deliberated. *What is he trying to infer?*

Tabitha moved from inside her cage out of the corner of my eye, facing me for the first time since our captor showed his face. Her eyes bore into my side, and I knew she had figured out this man's true intentions.

"*Marked Ones* have a gifted power given directly from the *Creator*; they can see auras and one's soul. That is all I know," I said with precision, staring into his soulless eyes.

My answer satisfied him, a contented smile greedily stretched across his face as he stood, making his way to the staircase hidden in the stone.

"Wait, my question!" I shouted, watching as he reluctantly turned back around.

"Go on with it."

"What is your name?"

He paused, clicking his tongue while thinking up a response.

"My name? What good would that do you?" He appeared inches before my face in seconds, gripping my jaw with his fingers. The bars did nothing to prevent him from hurting me. But the ancient magic that bound me to this cage rippled across the metal, searing his arm. The fool ignored the pain; his glare filled with pure cold hatred. "You wish to curse me as you lie there wasting away in your cage? You pathetic weakling."

He ripped his grip from my jaw, shaking his arm and hissing.

I rubbed my jaw, the pain pulsating into my ears. He stood, glowering at me from above as tears filled my eyes. I was thankful for the bars between us.

His mask had fallen, and he was the embodiment of hatred.

"My name is Ein." There was venom in his voice as it cut through the thick air between us. "Knowing my name won't change your fate, foolish girl." A sharp knife appeared in his hand, and he ran the blade against the iron bars, the irritating sound of metal scraping against metal echoing off the cavern walls.

There was an intensity that filled the air, filling the space in my lungs until my airway constricted. His true self was seeping out between the cracks of the black parasitic magic that continuously moved up and down the length of his figure. The treacherous man was testing me, waiting to see how I would respond.

I clenched my jaw shut, unflinching at his scare tactics.

After waiting for some time for me to speak, he then sauntered off into the shadows, the look of his dissatisfaction fading from my view.

Relief was evident as I inhaled a deep breath, holding a hand to my heart. I no longer had to pretend to be strong and put on an act for the monster's sake. His threat had gone dry in my mouth, and a cold sweat lined my skin.

When I was sure he was no longer there, I made an effort to relax the tension in my shoulders. Tabitha moved in her cage, and I turned to face her with a smile plastered on my face that still throbbed with a dull ache.

"His name is Ein," I crooned to her, the corners of my mouth turning upwards. "This is just the beginning. His sanity is unraveling at the seams."

Tabitha stared at me, unmoving, before shaking her head. "You should prioritize your sanity, Ornella." She crawled to the edge of the cage, gripping the metal bars. With her index finger, she beckoned me forward. "He wanted to know if you had been in contact with your sister."

"What? How?" It was my turn to stare at her incredulously. "The *Ligação Mágica* doesn't extend to inside the cavern. There's no way to cast a spell or use it to communicate through wavelengths."

She scoffed, waving her hand in the air as if none of what I said mattered.

"You are *Marked Ones* who lived in harmony together. Your bonds must be unbreakable. I'm surprised you two hadn't figured this out on your own. *Marked Ones* do not need the magic to communicate with each other. You need a strong soul connection, and your tendrils of light will do the rest."

I raised my brows and jumped to my feet as I began pacing my small quarters.

"Why didn't you mention this to me earlier? I could have tried to communicate with my sister this entire time." I side-eyed Tabitha, who met my glare with one of her own.

"I thought the magic that keeps us sealed inside these cages kept us from communicating with the outside. But that vile man's actions prove otherwise." She smirked, staring down at the *Breeders* and their army. "He's scared you will give up vital information to your twin. And he has every right to be." Tabitha's smile now reached her eyes, and something like a fire lit inside her crystal blue irises.

"To think I had given up hope. We still have a *Marked One* on the outside. Maybe there's still a chance."

Chapter Sixteen

Nox

It was as if I were staring at the shell of the woman I once knew. She lay there beneath the sheets, her body still. I observed her from the doorway for several seconds, picturing her face full of life as her smile crinkled her eyes. I shook the thought away and approached the bed, easing my weight onto its edge. My hand acted independently, brushing the few strands of greying hair away from her hollowed face.

"Mom?" I whispered, a pain emitting from my chest.

When was the last time I called out to her?

It must have been when I was a boy, and she still possessed her markings. Guilt traveled through me, my hand hesitating mid-air before withdrawing completely. I had avoided her room like it was a plague for many lunations, starting when I came of age and readily entered the sparring matches.

Something inside me shifted, and I now gravitated to her side as of late, and I dare say I would briefly witness a flicker in her demeanor, the warm luminescent glow returning to her cheeks and lips in the midst of her decaying *Gavinhas*. Tabitha had reassured me in my mourning when she was here in Alun; she was still alive, the tendrils of light weaving a cocoon of comfort around her fragile figure, cradling her as a mother would a child.

That alone brought me great comfort, knowing she was fighting to live, her soul protecting her body and shielding her from further agony.

Another wave of fault surfaced again, and my throat bobbed as tears pulled at the corners of my eyes.

What pain she must have endured for the sake of my father and our species' way of life. There were three options for a werewolf: to fight and win, to fight and lose, or to refuse and watch the soul suffer. The first option was what I chose, unknowingly continuing this monotonous way of life. Yes, I had respect, but I had also made many enemies in the process. I was next in line to inherit it all: the power, the land, and the responsibility. *What would have become of me if I had chosen to fight the system, like Silas had?* He was hated by most, but was free from the markings that bound us and our kind. The moon did not give or take from him, and I envied my best friend for having the backbone to choose his path, regardless of whether he realized it.

I became aware of how tense my body was; fangs protruded from my mouth. Thinking of the past brought out the beast within, along with several regrets. My attention flickered to my mother, and I managed to relax at the sound of her leveled breathing, one of the only signs she was still with us.

Her chambers were the same back then, from the single-family portrait displayed on the dresser to the room overtaken by the off-white hue. The bland color was what I associated with death; its underwhelming presence as it took a soul from this life to the next.

That was where my fear stemmed from—life faded in and out of existence without so much as a warning, a blaring sign to let loved ones know of their oncoming demise.

I questioned whether my blurry memories of her were, in fact, real, and if I had indeed experienced her hugs and laughter in the past. *Did we spend time in the orchards, tending to the crops and sneaking some ripe grapes in the midsummer evenings as the sun faded behind the hills? Was our time in the kitchen baking treats before our traditional supper with the clan at the end of harvest all a lie? Did my subconscious create fake memories to cope with reality?*

My mother's love was swept out from under me, and I was but a child in a room full of souls depending on me to lead without knowing how to nurture or care for anything other than my survival.

I unclenched my jaw, releasing a haggard breath.

The memories of my childhood had all but faded, and a fresh wave of sadness burrowed into my heart as I mourned the art of remembering.

I glanced out the window, the land's magic swirling about the greenery outside. The pit of anger burrowed deep in my chest awoke suddenly as I remembered the day she was first brought to this chamber. She had lost a match against the rival clan, the Bloodmoon Shadows, and as a young child, I watched in horror as the moonlight shone bright on her skin, so hot that she screamed in pain as her tribal markings withered away. They transferred to her opponent, the partner of their chief at the time. I'd never forget the wicked, cruel smile on the woman's face as she whispered something in my mother's ear, causing her to sob uncontrollably in the middle of the arena.

There was more to the story. The truth was palpable, and it was a vital reason why I hated my father. He refused to tell me the whole truth, though I had begged him countless times. Never had I heard of a being's *Gavinhas* slowly wane and disappear from heartache. It wasn't possible.

If my mother were to simply wake, she could tell me everything.

And I hated myself for feeling bitter toward her, for all of the precious memories missed out on. It was not her fault, yet the grudge festered inside me, growing profusely until I stopped visiting her. I was more than grateful for Odette, who cared for her as if she were her mother. I would never be able to repay my debt to the odd girl, the clumsy and defiant teen who was set on fighting in the arena at the next full moon.

I skimmed my mother's frame, and sparse from the lack of color, she looked as though she would wake at any instant.

"Demetria," I called out her name, the syllables foreign and heavy on my tongue. "I'm sorry it's taken me this long to visit. It's just...hard." My vision blurred, and I shifted my focus to the bedframe. "It's hard seeing you here like this, and knowing that this is how I think of you. I can't remember what it once was."

The bed creaked as I stood, going to stand between her and the window, creating a shadow over her figure.

"I'm talking with the chief and finding out why you are in this state. I will do everything I can to free you from your broken heart and save Tabitha." As soon as the statement left my mouth, it dawned on me that she didn't know. She had been in this perilous state for so long that my mother had no way of knowing her daughter had been imprisoned by the *Breeders of Thereon* in Mount Auberon.

My mother loved Tabitha from the second she was discovered as a small child on our shoreline without so much as a name of her own. Their bond was close—I'd say closer than anyone of blood. Their souls were intertwined and bound by love and acceptance. Linking the two of their *Gavinhas* together through the *Ligação Mágica* might be the answer to our woes.

It would be my sister if anyone were to be successful in waking her from her endless sleep.

"I do not fear my death, but the idea that I may never create another happy memory with you haunts me every day. So, please, wake up when I bring your daughter to you." I left her with the soft plea, unable to stay by her side for fear the armor I built around my exterior would crumble, revealing a small boy broken by his past.

Though my body moved and left the room, part of me stayed there at her side, quietly weeping and confessing the thoughts I did not dare to express out loud.

The pitter-patter of rain softly drummed on the windowsill, obscuring the view of those tending to the fields and beyond, as they dashed for cover on the other side. This was the only room in the manor that held any vibrancy; my father's art collection was dispersed throughout the area, littered with artifacts and vases that my mother had crafted with her hands in her youth. Earlier, I had felt confident, striding into the room to demand answers, believing this time would be different.

This time, my father, the chief, would suddenly change his mind and spill all of our family's secrets. He would reveal what happened to Mother, why she was stuck in this curse-like state. Standing here before him, I knew that I had been a fool, and I should've discussed with Silas how to approach the conversation with a man made without feeling.

"What you're asking for, son, isn't something I can give you," he croaked; his voice hoarse from constantly barking orders at others. "She should've woken up by now. It doesn't make sense." Papers spilled off the desk he sat behind and onto the floor; I almost felt sorry for him as he frantically sifted through the piles as if what he wanted would magically appear out of thin air. Almost.

"Drop the façade. I'm not a kid anymore. I've figured out enough to know Mom lost more than just her markings that night." I said through a clenched jaw, grinding my teeth. "I can't help her or Tabitha until you tell me everything."

My father paused, looking me over with his sharp eyes. His mane was disheveled, and the grey in his beard more prominent than I remember. A large exhale released from his lungs, and he leaned back in his leather chair, a quizzical expression painted onto his features.

"There's a forbidden magic that can heal your mother, and rid the five kingdoms of Aksel of the *Thereon* and their *Breeders.*"

"No type of magic like that exists." I dug my claws deeper into my biceps, desperate to hold on to my composure. It took everything in me not to deck the old man. "I want to know what happened that night. The last time I saw her, she was crying in the middle of the arena. Next thing I know, you send a random maid to my room to tell me she's sick and asleep."

The disinterest in his demeanor had boiled over, years of pent-up rage simmering beneath the surface. Anger spread throughout my body like a wildfire, its flames consuming the rest of my patience. I slightly crouched, assuming a fighting stance.

"*Answer me!*" The words ripped from my throat as I flexed my claws. I anticipated he would fight me right then and there, in his beloved study.

The sound of wood scraping the floor pierced my ears as my father abruptly stood, his arms crossed. He had no intention of sparring; instead, I was met with a deep-set frown paired with his steady glare.

"It does exist. Your mother believed in this magic and our cause."

"No." I shook my head slowly, in awe of his ability to blatantly ignore my questions. He had always been this way, hearing only what he wanted to, sharing information when it benefited him and his motives.

I pointed a finger at my father's chest. "She believed in *you.* She would've done anything *you* asked of her, because she loved *you.* Not the magic, not our clan, it was always *you* she wanted to impress, to prove her worth as the chief's chosen partner."

My hands gripped the edge of his desk, claws digging into the luxurious wood.

"If you loved her half as much as you love the title of being the chief, she would be here with us now. Awake, not tucked away in a stuffy room, and able to defend herself. I'm sure of it," I spat, ripping my hands from the table and swiftly turning to the door.

"Son, I'm warning you," he growled, his patience growing thin. "That night, your mother tried to recreate a weapon that the original *Marked Ones* once forged. She had been desperate to prove her worth to the clan, to me. I shouldn't have let her try. I should've stopped her." A muffled cry escaped his mouth, and his shoulder sank in defeat. "Now my Demetria is gone."

"She's still here!" I rounded the corner of his desk and pushed his chest with my fists, not holding back on my strength. My body shook with rage as I watched my father awkwardly collide with his armchair before he sank to the ground. "If you cared so much about her, why is she rotting away in that room? Why don't you visit her?" I no longer held back, the veins in my arms bulging.

"Your mother gave away too much of her soul that night. She'll never wake again. *Not until you find the soul shield.*" Strands of his greying hair shook in front of his face, and a crazed look glazed over his features.

"I do not believe in ridiculous fairytales. If such a weapon existed, the *Thereon* would have been defeated." I turned to the door, suffocated by the weighted intensity in the study. "I'll uncover the truth. *All of it.* I'll do everything you are too cowardly to try."

I squared my shoulders as I left, the entryway doors swinging behind me as the Fangs of the Fallen's chief sat crumpled on the floor.

For the first time in his life, my father was silent.

Chapter Seventeen

Sayah

The cheers of the onlookers stung more than the pain emitting from every inch of my body as I was thrown to the ground, an animalistic scream erupting from my mouth. I was in the middle of the arena, in a fight with the one being I had been desperate to avoid. Caelan stood over me, wearing a smirk along with her black leather tights and cropped shirt. The wound on my side had barely healed, and yet here I was, my arm pinned behind my back as she pushed my face further into the dirt.

"Yield," she commanded, digging her elbow between my shoulder blades.

I grunted, my cheeks burning with embarrassment. Out in the crowd behind several heads, I spotted Enid and Brom, their brows both knit together with worry. A flash of pink obscured my vision, and Kazumi was instantly in front of me, her razor-sharp teeth exposed as she grimaced.

"*Get. Up,*" the feisty fairy snarled, not willing to let me admit defeat.

I closed my eyes, trying to concentrate. Kazumi was a mastermind at getting under my skin, but she did not pity me the way everyone else did. When others sympathized with me about my misfortune, she got angry, not letting me use it as a crutch. And I would never tell her this, but I was grateful for her hot temper—occasionally.

I wiggled out of Caelan's grasp just as her hold on my arm began to slip, and I flipped onto my back, scrambling to stand. My physical training started several moons ago, and the only progress so far was the length of time before she had me on the ground, declaring defeat in front of everyone.

This had sparked rumors, nasty little things. I was a so-called esteemed *Marked One*, yet the daughter of Chief Bjorn, who had no powers at all, easily overcame me. What the werewolves failed to understand was that I did not want to fight or be blessed by the *Creator*. I didn't ask for this.

Bless the vine, all I wanted was to read books indoors and drink hot tea in the mornings.

I didn't want to grow my muscles and learn how to overtake an opponent in a match. But what I desired didn't matter, something I kept failing to remind myself. Ornella needed my saving, and she was worth me having a few scrapes and bruises, and whatever else is thrown my way.

Caelan lowered her body, her hands ready at her sides. My hands shook, anticipating her attack, and I tightened them into fists, ready to defend my vital spots. Her eyes never left mine as we stalked each other in a circle. She embodied a warrior in every aspect, from her precise movements to the way she carried herself. The young woman commanded respect. This was what she was born for, and what I should aspire to be as a *Marked One*.

I envied her for being given the space to grow into the best version of herself. This had never been an option for Ornella and me. Our existence was made up of lies from the instant we came into this world. We were born from a woman named Etienne, and because her love for us was so strong, she was willing to try to save us from a terrible fate. The elaborate scheme that we bloomed from, from *Videira*, to be accepted into the elven culture was not something I'm sure I would have chosen for myself.

My focus shifted to the crowd, where a familiar pair of russet eyes caused my heart to race. Nox was observing, but his facial expression did not indicate what he was thinking.

Caelan and Nox are the perfect match.

She struck my jaw with her fist, and a loud pop rang through my ears as the pain traveled from my head down my spine. I was on the floor again in an instant, with the weight of her body crushing me.

"Yield, or I'll end up breaking your bones," she growled her warning into my ear.

The taste of iron filled my mouth, and I licked my lips. *Bless the vine,* she had busted my lip. I ran my tongue over my teeth, relieved they were all intact. My vision was dazed from the strength with which she hit me, and I couldn't help but think she had put all her strength into that punch because I was her opponent.

Somehow, the weight of her body shifted and began to constrict my airway. I desperately looked up at the crowd, their blurry faces shouting words I couldn't understand. I found Enid's face out of the masses; her warm brown eyes filled with concern as she shook her head.

"I yield," I croaked, and the weight holding me hostage vanished.

The sounds of rejoicing filled the air, and I turned over on my back in the dirt, closing my eyes to focus on taking steady breaths. When I opened them again, Caelan stood over me, her hand extended. Heat rose to my cheeks as I took her hand, and she helped me up to my feet.

"You're improving," she skimmed over my figure before adding, "Next time, quit staring at Nox and you might stand a chance. Maybe."

"How can you tell?" I asked, raising a brow and simultaneously wiping blood from my chin with the back of my hand.

"You're starting to anticipate my movements, but you're not quick enough yet to block my jabs or be on the offensive side yet," Caelan retorted, and I observed from the corner of my eye as the crowd shifted to the next two beings about to begin their training nearby.

"Good, they're leaving." The words slipped out from my thoughts, and Caelan barked a laugh.

"You get used to it after fighting in the arena several times." Her vision went hazy as she stared off into the distance. "Ignore them, and they'll stop messing with you. Understand?"

I nodded, and her focus returned to reality just in time to see her father standing alongside Chief Phoenix underneath the manor's porch, just outside his office. The two leaders seemed to be having a heated discussion, their voices sharp as the wind carried their undecipherable words.

"See you at dawn, *Marked One*." She nudged my shoulder. "Go get yourself cleaned up in the meantime."

I watched her jog ahead, entering through the vineyard. Caelan's half-shaved head revealed black swirls that decorated her skull, and who knows how many fights she won to have those tribal markings. As she approached the entryway, she was greeted by several werewolves with open arms. She had earned that respect over years of training. Their expressions were hardened, and as they greeted Caelan, patting her back with approval, I could feel the intensity of their stares as I awkwardly stood in the middle of the arena. Pain still ebbed and flowed from my head, a splitting headache emerging.

The afternoon faded into the evening, and I didn't feel like returning to my room, not after being punched square in the jaw in front of the entire clan. I aimlessly wandered through the rows of crops, stopping short at a fence post lining the property.

Despite the beings in this kingdom not taking a liking to me, I was beginning to feel content with my surroundings. Sure, a lot of werewolves weren't fans, but that reaction was to be expected anywhere I went. However, they did respect my privacy, and some were not shy about approaching me when I passed them in the corridors.

This place was different from Erebus, where I had taken an immediate liking to the creatures there, the winter wonderland glazing over all my concerns. I already missed Ulfred, the giant werewolf that was my *mãe's* soulmate.

Mãe. Oh, how my heart still ached for her every day.

I often wondered what she would do if she were in my shoes and what advice she would give. Sometimes, I would wake up in the early mornings, half expecting to smell lemon tea wafting into my bedroom and Ornella softly snoring beside me. My heart would drop to the pit of my stomach when I was met with the smell of lavender and the bland white walls of the manor.

I yearned for the life I had when my concerns consisted of my music sheets and how I would take over *Mãe's* music academy after the rite of passage.

"What's wrong with me?" I confessed in a single breath, desperate to hold on to the present as I gazed over the rolling hills. The evanescent sunset tugged at some long-forgotten emotion buried deep within the shadows, where I had hidden the memories of my past, both the good and the evil. Any memory that evoked too much feeling resided there, protected by the armor I built for myself brick by brick. But life was amusing in that way, and as soon as you prepare never to let in another soul, a group of unlikely misfits comes along and wears down your armor. "I am heartbroken *because* I am happy. And every time, what's left of my shattered heart aches. It doesn't heal."

It was then quiet, other than the sounds of the wind running its fingertips along the tall grass and an occasional bird chirping overhead. The orange and pink sky melded into one and faded into the unknown.

I felt his presence appear. He hesitated for several beats beside me before leaning over the fence, using his forearms to prop himself up on the wooden post.

"That feeling never leaves you. It will always tug at you, a reminder in the back of your mind that they are gone." In that moment, the sunset reflected in Nox's eyes, a solemn smile playing at the edge of his lips. "She would want you to laugh, Sayah. To experience the feeling of life's burdens momentarily lifted from your soul, your heart swimming in happiness."

Bells chimed from the estate, interrupting our thoughts, signaling that the day had come to an end. His shoulders suddenly tensed, his features hardening as he focused on something in the distance. "Drown yourself in it, because I can't promise it will return anytime soon."

Nox's reaction made my entire body stiffen, my heart accelerating as I turned to face his home. There was a feeling of friction in the air, and I found myself preparing for a different fight this time as we headed back to the manor for the evening.

When I saw Silas emerge from the front entryway, his expression confirmed that I would not be getting a wink of sleep tonight.

Chapter Eighteen

Sayah

S ilas rushed out to greet us, throwing a cloak over my shoulder. The atmosphere intensified the instant I stepped through the doorway; the shadows cast by the moonlight about the room were no longer a comforting blanket to hide away in, but ominous. Staff members were out of sight, the stillness of the usual lively manor unsettling. Nox had placed his arm around me, his russet irises glowing. Orbs of light briefly traveled along his tribal markings and up his neck. Something was off, that much, I was sure. Goosebumps traveled up my spine as we made our way to the foot of the stairs, and I abruptly craned my neck to view the magic, to perceive its current state—it moved about freely, the gentle green and gold swirls stretching their limbs toward the doorway before Silas stood in front of me, blocking my view.

"Nox, you are needed in the dining room." A visible muscle in his jaw twitched, and he was then leading me up the staircase. "Keep them in there for as long as you can, and meet where I told you to."

I twisted my body in the direction my heart told me to follow, desperate to go to him. But Nox shook his head, his hand reaching for mine resting on the banister. Without hesitation, I met his grasp, my fingers running over his skin to memorize each and every callus, the warmth he possessed.

"I'll see you soon." There was a longing in his voice that made my throat tighten. He nodded to Silas, who was impatiently waiting for our goodbye to end. "What am I up against this time?"

"It's not what—it's *who*." Silas tugged me up the flight of stairs, only briefly stopping to look down at Nox once we were at the top. He side-eyed me before speaking, careful to choose his following words. "Unexpected guests are talking with all four chiefs at the moment. Why don't you go and stir up some trouble, like always?"

They both grinned, and a knowing look gleamed in Nox's eyes.

"Stirring up trouble is the one thing I'm good at." He winked and then disappeared down the corridor.

"What's going on?" I whispered, the urgency in my tone evident. Silas's figure was stiff as we both walked briskly down the narrow hallway leading to my chambers.

"We are leaving tonight. Odette is preparing a bath for you in your room as we speak, and has picked an outfit for you to wear." His voice grew soft, and a sadness lingered in his golden irises. "You must be quick, Sayah. Your fate is being decided as we speak."

Wha—" A hand covered my mouth, and we both froze.

The sound of muffled voices emitted from the adjacent room as the entryway opened, revealing two figures hidden by the shadows of night. Silas pulled up the hood of the cloak just in time to hide my identity.

"We cannot afford for you to anger their chief, Josias." The unknown being murmured, an undercurrent of warning lacing their words.

"Our *Videira* is on our side, Elder Calwen. The sacred vine always provides."

That voice. The unwarranted confidence. My body began to shake, fear constricting my lungs. *He couldn't be here. It isn't possible.* Tears pulled at the corners of my eyes, blurring my vision.

Elves rarely left Alizeh. They did not travel far from the *Videira*, their source of life. It went against their nature and beliefs to leave the kingdom for more than a few moons at a time.

We moved ahead, my feet heavy as we entered my chamber and shut the door behind us.

"The elders came for me," I said in a daze, the ringing in my ears growing in volume. "I can't believe it."

Silas nodded, his features solemn. "That is why we are leaving. Nox is keeping our guests entertained long enough for you to prepare for our quick departure from Alun. We depart for Adara tonight, Sayah."

"Tonight?" Shock coursed through me, my legs going weak. I managed to catch myself on my mattress, and I anxiously began to bite my nails. "I'm not ready, Silas. I haven't mastered hand-to-hand combat, and I'm still a disaster when it comes to controlling my gift. I can't leave."

My friend rested his hands on both my shoulders, and I hesitantly met his gaze.

"But you must. We are never ready for what life throws our way. For what hand we have been dealt. The only choice we have is to choose how we react during the difficult times. When you decide to keep fighting when the most obvious choice would be to give in to the pressure, that is what makes you strong. That is what defines a true warrior."

I studied the hardness of his face and the fading scar that traveled from his brow and across his left eye, a reminder of the time when they were still in their adolescence and on the cusp of adulthood, given to him by Nox.

He was the epitome of inner strength. No markings to prove his worth, yet here Silas stood before me, without so much as a fragment of hesitation. His *Gavinhas* were bright, unwavering.

I decided to trust him because I could not trust myself to follow through, not after seeing Elder Josias here in the flesh. There was still so much I needed to improve on, and my mind was not the fortitude it required.

I must protect my tendrils of light at all costs to keep our plans hidden from enemies on all fronts.

And the *Ligação Mágica* was no longer a dependency I could afford to rely on or trust.

"Leave. I'll be ready before you can tie both shoelaces." I gestured to the door with my chin.

"No, we need more time than that." Odette appeared at my feet, tugging my boots off in haste. "I'll shove her out the door after I've helped scrub the grime off. Who knows when your next bath will be?"

"Understood." Silas moved to the door and opened it slightly as he peered over his shoulder to look back. "We don't have much time. Alizeh's army is beginning to set up camps around the perimeter of the Fangs of the Fallen's territory. They'll go to war over you."

"I get it, no need for the emphasis. Now shoo." I waved him out of my chamber, and Odette immediately began to rip my garments off. "I can get changed myself!" I huffed and began to shuffle through the clothes she had laid out on my mattress. "This is—"

"Our clan's fighting gear. It's the least I could do for someone as hopeless as you in the ring." Her tone was matter-of-fact as she clicked her tongue in disapproval, scanning the cuts and bruises going up and down my appendages.

"I don't know whether I should whack you on the head or thank you," I quipped, sticking my tongue out at her as I finished undressing.

"Just say thank you and hop into the bath I've so graciously prepared." She shoved me into the bathing quarters—the suds already having dissipated into the lukewarm water.

I winced at the bath's temperature, sliding into the tub and watching Odette immediately begin to scrub a day's worth of filth from my arms. A pang of longing struck a chord in my chest as we both sat in the silence.

This reminded me of my rite of passage, and *Mãe* scrubbing the day's trek to the *Videira* off my skin. I looked down at my hands, and they trembled beneath the soapy surface. *Moonflower*, her gentle voice took shape in my mind. I pictured her in Odette's stead; her blonde hair wrapped into a tight bun on the top of her head as she worked. I missed the way her violet eyes would crinkle when she laughed, and the melody that radiated from her being. She was the embodiment of music itself, living and breathing. It felt as though music had died when *Mãe's* soul was no longer tethered to our world.

A splash of water to my face brought me out of my daze, and I narrowed my eyes as Odette was oblivious to my change in mood, pouring a bucket of water over my head.

"What are you thinking about?" she quipped, throwing a rag at me. "Start helping me as you answer. Clean your face, there's dirt on your chin."

"Bless the vine, that's wonderful," I replied, sarcasm laced in each word. "Nox saw me with dirt all over my face. Why didn't anyone tell me?" My face flushed as I recalled the touch of his hand in mine. "Do you want to go with us?"

The instant I uttered the question, I knew it wasn't feasible. I saw her for more than her age, but she had yet to come of age in her clan and had no fighting experience whatsoever. The blaring truth was I was being selfish, and I did not want her to leave my side. I was scared of losing yet another being I cared for.

She paused, soap suds dripping onto the tile outside the tub.

"I can't." She held out a hand to me, helping me stand. "There's someone here who needs me more than you do." I glanced down at my abdomen, the bright red mark a stark reminder of what I had endured.

And that's when it occurred to me: the strange woman in the bedroom down the hall. How she remained a relic in time was no coincidence. Someone had to have been caring for her.

"It was ridiculous of me to ask." I shrugged and started to dry my skin, standing over my new attire sprawled out on the bedding. "I can't thank you enough, Odette." A lump formed in my throat, tears threatening to fall to the floor below.

I felt movement around my waist and looked down to see her delicate hands wrapping a bandage around my mark.

"One last time. To be cautious and because knowing you, you'll somehow reinjure yourself." She cinched the fabric tight, meeting my gaze. "You've trained with Caelan for almost a whole lunation, and I've witnessed your improvements."

I nodded, unable to reply with words. The uniform was made of a surprisingly breathable black leather that completely covered my figure. A new pair of shoes had also been placed at the foot of the bed, and I picked them up to feel the heels of the fabric. They were stiff, unworn. Lacing on the combat boots awkwardly, my fingers fumbled with the strings.

I didn't feel ready. But was there ever a point in time that I had?

I felt a hand on my shoulder, and Odette's voice was soft and urgent. "I will see you again, Sayah." She squeezed, and I looked up from my kneeling position to meet her hazel irises. "Let me repeat myself, I *will* see you again, and I'll get to meet your sister, whom you steal treats from, even though she is an awful baker and she can't make any to replenish for herself."

A smile tugged at the corners of my mouth, and I patted Odette on the back.

"Precisely. You'll get the pleasure of meeting my better half."

Chapter Nineteen

Nox

The shadows on the walls seemed to swallow me whole as I crossed the threshold into the dimly lit dining room, where hushed voices and the scent of burning candles greeted me at the entryway. My father sat at the head of the table, and at his side were the three chiefs from the other clans. Everyone important was here. Unwelcome guests were seated adjacent to several clan members; their elongated, sharply pointed ears, along with the green and gold armor, immediately gave away their identity.

"Why are they here?" My voice split through the foreboding stillness. Several heads snapped in my direction, and the leaders of the elven army did not hide their disdain at my presence as I sat next to Chief Hoku of the Bloodmoon Shadows. His height matched his temper, alongside the thick bleached brows, their high arches giving him the most fitting expression.

"Bout time you showed your face," he grumbled, smacking me on the backside. "You've traveled enough. Take your spot at the head of the table, Nox, and lead like you were born to do."

I grimaced, my focus shifting to where my father sat, unenthused.

On his left, Chief Tariq sat completely still, observant. In my opinion, if anyone were to overthrow my father's leadership in the four clans, it would be that man. His eyes were sharp, and he spoke with an eloquence that my father had never mastered. Perhaps that is why they were seated directly next to one another, because keeping your enemies close was an often-used strategy. I took a mental note to keep an eye on the Crimsonclaw Howlers' movements and to see what they've been working up behind the scenes.

"But Hoku, I've been enjoying myself out at sea. And I don't think I'm ready for such a big commitment." I glanced sideways at the short-fused man, his complexion a shade of crimson. He was the perfect decoy to toy with, distracting the unwanted guests and my father so that Sayah could sneak past her betrayers.

This was not who I expected when Silas said there were house guests. Elven leaders, accompanied by several soldiers, sat but a few feet away.

"It's Chief Hoku, to you." He then grunted, shifting his focus. "When can we begin the negotiations?"

"We are waiting on a few more guests," the elven man sitting directly in front of Chief Bjorn answered. His figure was slender, and he had a long, straight nose. Two other elders sat on either side, their robes adorned with patches that displayed their status and rank. I did not care for their snobbish culture, but now I wish I had inquired what the odd symbols meant sewn into the emerald fabric from Sayah.

"What is being negotiated?" I side-eyed Hoku, whose body weight shifted ever so slightly in the direction of my father. He sat unmoving, the look of annoyance etched across his features. This fact alone made me frown, because he was only serious if his beloved hierarchy was at stake. "Hoku, answer an old friend." I nudged him with my elbow. "What is—"

The entryway doors flew open before I could finish, and two more guests entered the room. Their robes were tan, the traditional garment stopping short at their ankles. Both elders' chests and shoulders were decorated in symbols, and the air in which they held themselves let me know everything I needed to know about these blowhards. "Elder Josias!" The elven military exclaimed in unison as they bowed, showing respect. None of the werewolves moved an inch, and the room was instantly thick with tension.

"Hello, my brethren. May the *Videira* bless you and your families. I know this journey away from our sacred vine must have been difficult, but given the circumstances, it is necessary for all of Elven kind." Each word that spewed from Elder Josias' mouth was unintentionally sweet, and from the look in the eyes of those who adored him, they ate it up like candy. "Let us begin." He then motioned to the entire room, and those who stood for his presence sat back in their seats.

Elder Josias and his companion sat in the last two chairs available and rested their hands in a praying position at their chests. The other elders followed suit, mimicking his movements.

"Well then. Why are you here?" my father questioned, his tone lacking any enthusiasm.

"The army of Alizeh is here to retrieve the property of our kingdom, the last remaining *Marked One* inside the five kingdoms. She is named Sayah, daughter of Aster."

I wasn't sure who had said it, because the moment they called Sayah their property, all I could see was red. My fangs protruded in response, and I fought to keep my grip on my claws from extending.

Now was not the time for me to lose my temper, I repeated to myself. If I wanted to help Sayah and Silas escape Alun without being detected, it was essential that I remain calm and not react emotionally. At least, not yet.

I flexed my fingers and focused on taking long, deep breaths.

The silence that followed was uncomfortable, and the growing tension inside the dining hall became palpable. The soldiers shifted uncomfortably, the elders clasping and unclasping their hands. We had arrived at the crossroads quicker into the discussion than I expected, but that's precisely when I had an epiphany.

"What right do you have to come all the way here to our kingdom and request that one of our guests be taken against their will?" I leaned over the dark wood, my heart racing. The four chiefs grunted in unison, agreeing with my statement. *Good.* The hair on the back of my neck rose, and I leaned back into the leather chair, a smile playing at the corners of my mouth.

"Sayah is the property of—"

"What makes her the property of Alizeh? Please, delight all of us here in this room and explain how exactly she is labeled as your possession." I challenged, cutting one of the elders off, and I immediately held their attention as they stared daggers at me.

"She is an elf; she bloomed from the vine of life, the *Videira*. Sayah is a *Marked One* and our responsibility," Elder Josias snapped, losing brief control of his calm demeanor. His sweet words had turned sour, and I saw the snake for what he was—a conniving man with ill intentions.

A grin spread across my face, and I cocked a brow. "Based on your definition, Sayah is not an elf. She did not, in fact, bloom from the *Videira*. She is not, by your description, one of your species, and therefore is not your property. Not that anyone should ever be viewed as property; at least, we do no such thing here in the kingdom of Alun."

Elder Josias' eyes bulged, and we all witnessed the color drain from his complexion. The elves seated at the table were frozen in place, and I kicked my feet up onto the table, smug with my discovery.

The elders were unaware that Sayah knew the truth, that she and Ornella did not bloom from their sacred vine.

"You lie to deceive my kind; that is preposterous!" The snake disguised as a man pointed his wrinkled fingers at my chest, with hate oozing from every inch of his existence.

"If she is not an elf, then this does indeed prove to be a predicament," Chief Bjorn spoke, rubbing his chin, speculating. "Phoenix, how should we proceed?"

Hearing my father's name, I squinted at him with intent. *Surely, he would take the bait that I practically handed him, and he will refuse negotiations with such pompous blowhards. Surely.* But as I took in his cold, calculating stare and his unnervingly calm approach to the absurd request, all hope dissipated from my body.

"The four clans will honor our original agreement." He nodded once, and the Elders' shoulders relaxed, the tension leaving their expressions.

"You allow us to perform our ritual, and we will then return her to your custody."

"And you remove the spell placed on her *Gavinhas*." One of the elves added, raising his brows. "We do not know how to remove the complex spell, and unfortunately, it has made tracking her whereabouts difficult."

Heat rushed to my face, and my limbs began to shake as I clenched the edge of the table. They wanted the spell derived from our species, *Escudo das Almas*, removed from Sayah's *Gavinhas*. We had cast the magic around her tendrils of light to form a protective barrier from unwanted invaders. Other species used the *Ligação Mágica* as a means to spy on their kind and keep track of their every move. And the Elven army would have no trouble tracking Sayah's location once the spell was no longer there to protect her.

I couldn't let that happen; she would be their prisoner indefinitely.

"We're agreed, then," Chief Hokus grumbled, and he pushed his chair backwards, reading his exit.

"No, we are *not* finished," I growled, baring my teeth. "Explain. What ritual?"

My father rubbed his forehead, sighing. The rest of the room waited in anticipation for his explanation, caught between our dispute. "I told you, son. Your mother tried to perform it for us many lunations ago, and failed." He stroked his beard, lost in thought. "We realized we needed a *Marked One* to recreate the *soul shield*. If only we had known." The remnants of regret were sprinkled throughout his tone, his face momentarily downcast as his head bobbed.

"*The soul shield?* You mean that ridiculous children's tale, with the lore of a weapon so powerful it could heal any wound? Grant any wish? You can't be serious." I sank back into my chair, mystified. "You're selling a being with a living soul back to their captors, for an item that doesn't even exist."

"There was one, once, long ago. Before the world was split in two." All heads turned to Chief Tariq, whose voice was like a roaring river. Powerful, his words flowed effortlessly throughout the room. "And we can recreate that treasure again. Now that we have access to a *Marked One* that your partner is not attached to." His gaze flickered to my father, whose eyes were made of steel, cold and resolute.

"What?" I choked, staggering out of my chair. My body suddenly became heavy, there on the hard floor. "What did he just say?"

"The original plan was to use the *Marked One*, known to you as Tabitha, to recreate *the soul shield.* But your mother grew attached to her, and on the day of the ritual, she decided to intervene and take the *Marked One's* place." Tariq continued to speak, but my eyes could not leave my father's emotionless expression. "In an effort to conceal her from us, before performing the ritual, she had made plans with an unknown source to watch over Tabitha until she was able to sneak her out of Alun. And that ultimately is how Tabitha ended up in the clutches of the *Breeders of Thereon.* Your mother is to blame."

The truth drove straight through my chest, as if a dagger was fully plunged inside of me. Chief Tariq mercilessly twisted the blade, accusing my mother of being the reason for Tabitha's capture. I was now on my knees, tears of hatred blinding my vision.

"She was your partner; Tabitha is your daughter!" I screamed, the sound bouncing off the high, vaulted ceilings. "How could you betray your own family in this way? How could you?" My voice cracked, and a sob escaped from deep within my chest.

"I did no such thing!" he growled, jumping up from his seat at the head of the table. "It was for the greater good of our clan! For all four clans!" My father moved at a blinding speed; he was suddenly over top of me; his fingers pointed at my chest. "This is why you were never fit to lead the Fangs of the Fallen, my boy. You can't put others before our species' way of life; our survival. We tried to find the original *soul shield*. I've sent you out on your ridiculous escapades to see if you would happen upon it." He leaned into my ear while patting my back. "You did well, and you brought us back a *Marked One,* of all things. I'm proud of you."

Something inside me snapped; the remaining hope that my father could become a decent man came untethered.

"Now I know without a shred of doubt, I have failed." My hands rested limp on my thighs, the continuous stream of regret and anguish traveling down my cheeks. "Because you are the last being I would ever want to make proud." I forced my body to stand up, though the weight of the world was pressing down on my new reality. "I won't let you hurt Sayah the way you hurt mother. I won't let a single one of you touch a hair on her head!" My claws unsheathed, and the muscles in my arms protruded.

"You misunderstand once again." The Chief of the Fangs of the Fallen rested his hands behind his back and began to circle the table of the wide-eyed onlookers. "We do not intend to kill her. A *Marked One's Gavinhas* are strong enough to withstand the ritual, and have the *Creator's* blessing to mold their soul anew." His stroll around the rectangular table stopped when he happened upon a painting of the vineyard outside. "We waited for her wound to heal, son. She was fed, tended to, given a place to rest as well as fresh, clean garments to wear." My father then turned to face me, his eyes thoughtful. "Shouldn't she want to repay us for our kindness?

This is the least that the *Marked One* can manage. And she can travel back to her homeland and live with the beings she grew up with. This agreement between our two species makes the most sense."

"Precisely. This situation is greater than one being's free will. This choice will unite two kingdoms," Elder Josias murmured, content with the current resolution. He motioned for the Elders beside him to stand, and they bowed to my father before filing out of the room.

"I don't understand." I glared at the werewolves who were still present at the table, their faces shrouded in solitude. "Why do they insist on taking Sayah back to Alizeh?"

"That, Nox, is an easy answer," Chief Bjorn hummed, and he took a swig of his drink before slamming the mug down, rattling the utensils on the wooden surface. "*Marked Ones* are viewed as possessions by kingdoms, both weapons and shields, by outsiders. In their eyes, we stole their most valuable asset. Who knows what would have happened if we hadn't agreed to send her back with them?" His eyes shifted ever so slightly to my father, who was now standing on the far side of the room, conversing privately with Chief Tariq. "Perhaps there is more at stake than just your friend's freedom."

I gritted my teeth and checked myself once over to make sure I had, in fact, somehow kept my composure. *Good, Silas will be pleased.*

"Perhaps," I answered while popping my knuckles, preparing myself for the next round of insanity. "But I will do everything in my power to keep that from happening, Chief Bjorn."

He looked at me briefly and shrugged his shoulders. "Be my guest—see if you have what it takes to defeat two kingdoms' armies, all for a single girl."

"She's not just a girl, Bjorn—Sayah's my jewel. If anyone touches her without her consent, they can meet me out back for a nice chat," I threatened, my voice low. I headed out of the entryway to find the woman who was the keeper of all my affections.

Chapter Twenty
Ornella

When I close my eyes, I can see it. The clear sky overhead, as the sun's rays peek through the entangled branches, meeting my bare skin with its warmth. Mushrooms dance along the dirt path as I stroll by, welcoming my continuously coming and going presence. The sounds of the birds chirping and the woodland creatures scampering in the brush were a familiar comfort. Green and gold swirls flowed with a gentle ease along the earth, climbing into the trees and tickling the leaves. I could see our cottage, perfectly nestled into its surroundings, as if it were a part of nature itself, as if it had taken root in the soil and sprouted like the daffodils and daisies that had been plucked and placed on its windowsill.

And I could envision a head of wild raven hair, running ahead to catch up to *Mãe* as she passed underneath the traditional elvish carvings, the large crescent-shaped window illuminated by the candlelight inside.

Our tendrils of light had been tethered together from the instant of our birth into this world, and yet it always felt that Sayah was just out of reach, a few feet ahead of me in every way.

I opened my eyes; my vision blurred with tears. No longer inside my memories in the kingdom of Alizeh, I was met with rusted iron bars and shrieks of terror emanating from deep inside the caverns of Mount Auberon.

"Why can't I do it?" A sob rattled loose from my chest, and I twisted to face Tabitha in the cage adjacent to mine. "You said my connection with Sayah would be strong enough for me to reach her, without the help of the *Ligação Mágica.*"

Her sapphire eyes sparkled in the dim light as she drank in my expression, studying me as if the answer would suddenly come spilling out onto the rusted floor.

"You said you were twins, that grew from the same womb, yes?" she pondered, scratching the side of her head. "There must be a deviation in your bond—a snag. Something large enough to create a rift between the two of you."

My throat went dry. An image of Sayah, her eyes black as night in her torn ceremony dress, flashed in my vision.

"Yes, I would say there is tension in our relationship," I murmured, knowing that it was much more than a mere disagreement. She was my sister, the only flesh and blood I had, and I was terrified of her. I was terrified of her abilities, of what she could be capable of. And there was this festering wound growing in my heart, a negative emotion budding in silence. Sayah was with *Mãe* when she died, and she took no action. I knew it was wrong to blame her for what happened, but as I lay wasting away in my prison, the feelings had begun to ferment in my core, strangling what hope I had originally salvaged.

"Maybe if you were to try and communicate these unsaid thoughts or feelings, you could synchronize both of your *Gavinhas*." Tabitha shrugged her shoulders, sighing. "It's worth a shot. We have nothing else left to lose."

"I can think of one thing in particular." The thought was born from my lips, and I squinted past the bars, beyond the ancient blue magic crackling outside of our cages, and into the dark abyss. A flicker of a dull light glowed far in the distance, inside the center of the mountain.

We could lose our sense of self and the reason why we exist at all.

"We will not become *Thereon*, Ornella."

"What if what we become is worse?" I countered, my fingers clenching what was left of my trousers. The fabric was tattered, covered in a layer of filth. "We have yet to see what happens when a *Marked One* is turned using a *Breeder's* blood. Will our powers manifest in a corrupt way? I can't help but think this is a part of Bakunax's plan."

Tabitha sat up straight, her eyes widening. "I suppose that is something to mull over..." Her voice trailed off, and she rubbed her chin, considering. "I have my doubts on your theory. He wants to absorb our gifts and harness the power from a direct source. I can't picture him wanting to have to tend to too many puppets, and that leads to another question. What if turned *Marked Ones* require more of the *Breeder's* blood to be satiated than the average *Thereon?* What then?" She shook her head, crossing her arms. "His escape from Mount Auberon is what he desires most, at least at the moment. He's not going to jeopardize everything by potentially weakening his most valuable assets, not when he is so close to breaking free."

"And by valuable assets, you mean the other *Breeders*?" I placed my palms over my chest, cradling the unsteady thrumming emitting from inside.

"And their army of *Thereon*. Focus on what you can do, Ornella." She looked at me pointedly, the shadows framing the windows to her soul. "Try again. Reach out to Sayah using your bond; synchronize your wavelengths. Your tendrils of light know each other from the womb. There's a reason you two were brought into this world together."

"How can you possibly know that?" I asked, uncertain.

"I don't. I am just trying to motivate you. Now go on, and focus." Her tone reminded me of *Mãe's* when she insisted I keep baking, even after the cottage was filled to the brim with smoke and the charred remains of what was supposed to be a dessert rested on top of a pitiful grave of soot.

I sighed, my shoulders sagging.

Bless the vine, this will be my last time trying. I'm going to give it everything I have to reach her.

Sayah was hard to connect with, at least for me. This fact alone was difficult to acknowledge, because we were sisters. *Twins.* We were expected to have an unbreakable bond, one that would not bend at the slightest inconvenience, with a love that could transcend the space between us.

But the truth managed to seep its way out of the cracks, eventually boiling over until I had to face the undeniable reality: our bond had always been weak; a fragile piece of fabric, held together by what was left of its seams. And *Mãe* had been the thread, intertwining the two of our souls, our foundation.

And from the moment she died, that foundation started to crumble, withering away into nothing more than remnants of memories.

There was also another certainty, that whenever I was alone with my thoughts a moment too long, it would creep its way back into the forefront, invading space while depleting what little self-preservation I had left. A wickedness had planted its seed in my heart, festering and growing from the instant I was able to use my powers for the good of the villagers and the betterment of Alizeh.

How did I end up as the twin with the most expectations, while Sayah was allowed to practice the music that she loves, and wander the Woodlands free from the burden of the villagers' wants and desires? I had the ability to gift energy, not change one's fate.

It was this belief that had taken a tangible form, manifesting in the shadows of my mind, blooming from unrestrained jealousy.

How was I supposed to connect with Sayah, knowing this?

Tabitha cleared her throat, and my head swiveled in her direction, a flush spreading over my skin.

"Don't rush me; I'm starting," I chimed, straightening my spine while crossing my legs. My breathing slowed, and I let my eyes rest, my subconscious drifting into the dark.

I recalled who Sayah was to me before the day of our rite of passage. She was the daughter of the moon, a friend of winter, and the master of melody. There was a darkness bubbling beneath her fair exterior, rippling out of her in waves, like hands outstretched reaching into existence, desperate to find any form of light.

Without the *Ligação Mágica* to guide me, there was no tug on my *Gavinhas* to pull me in any clear direction. I was left to drift aimlessly through my memories, observing my sister through my own filtered narrative.

Sayah's figure would alternate between her elven form and that of a monster; her insidious eyes were pitch-black, the tendrils of light encompassing her void, where the fragments of her once-illuminated essence had vanished. She was now a stranger, no longer the sister I had grown to love and cherish.

It was too intense; my heart rate climbed as the panic set in.

I shook myself free of the images, and Tabitha's solemn face was once again across from me, and I was suddenly aware of how alone I was in that cage perched high inside the caverns of Mount Auberon.

There is no one connected to me; I do not have a bond with a single soul.

Fresh waves of despair came crashing down on my resolve, and I cradled my head in my hands, the sounds of anguish rolling out of my mouth as they echoed into the chaotic abyss.

"Ornella, do not cry," she coaxed, her voice growing in volume as she scooted across the metal floor. "We can try to reach her another time. For now, why don't you rest?"

"You don't understand." Another fit of sobs rattled my chest. "I am alone, Tabitha. I am more alone now than I have ever been. It's taken me this long to realize it." I sniffled, wiping my nose with my sleeve. "When *Mãe* died, I not only lost the most important being in my life; I lost the single connection my soul had with another. And I hate this; I hate that I am not who my sister needs me to be. The truth is, I am afraid of her. This fear has been in my heart and manifested in the womb, I believe. It is a part of who I am, and I cannot face her because of its existence."

My head pulsed as I lay in the fetal position, anticipating her reaction. But the quiet stretched across the space between us, depleting the air in my lungs.

"You are not alone, you have me, right here. And I can hear you rolling your eyes, by the way," she quipped, and I couldn't help the awkward fit of laughter that shook my chest.

Bless the vine, she is always spot on with her remarks. I was rolling my eyes.

"Connections can be broken, non-existent. But they can also be forged, mended. That's the beautiful thing about souls, Ornella. They are living, forever changing, never the same as the day before." Her voice grew soft, her intentions nearly palpable. "You can strengthen the bonds with those you love and care for. It is not one-sided. You can put in the effort to change the way your relationship is shaped with your sister."

My breathing hesitated, and it took several beats for the shock of her words to set in fully.

Am I the problem?

"You've given me much to think about. I think I'll take your advice and rest," I mumbled, rolling over to face the ancient rock formations, with the impending storm down below.

There were times that I forgot about the *Breeders* and their abominations, because I was so detached from reality. I felt as though I was no longer in a cage protected by an ancient magic, but instead I was frozen in time, left behind.

My hair fell limp over my line of sight as several whimpers escaped from my fragile figure. The cage beneath me shook, and it wasn't for some time that I realized it was I who was shaking, shivering on the cold surface.

Both my body and heart were numb, and Tabitha was silent.

Chapter Twenty-One

Tabitha

There's nothing quite like watching another being suffer. That was why I was convinced all the *Marked Ones* were held in separate cages, not out of convenience for our captors. It was another form of torture, one of the spirit. We were close enough to familiarize ourselves with our comrades' faces, and we were subjected to watching as their hope faded with the passing of each moon.

I sat with my back against the cage, staring at Ornella's delicate figure.

All I wanted in this moment was to comfort her, to tell her it would be okay, that I knew what it was like to have not a single soul on your side. I truly knew. There was no one before her. My memories were like freshly plucked wildflowers—beautiful yet fleeting. Destined to wither as time meandered forward. I could not recall who I was before I washed up on the shores of Alun, not even a name. Tabitha was given to me by my mother simply because she liked the way it sounded and thought it suited me well. That was another quirk I had loved about that odd woman; she accepted me as if I had grown in her belly and come from her womb the second we made eye contact.

The other *Marked Ones* were spaced a bit farther away, but I could hear their occasional moans of despair. Ornella was the last to arrive, the last to have the courage to fight for freedom, still breathing inside her core. I shouldn't have said what I said. She wasn't ready to confront the truth; what she needed was a friend who listened without casting judgment and helped to subside her current transgressions.

But the mistake had been made, even if my approach was gentle. Her slender form shook with despair, even as she slept. I hadn't taken the time to get to know her, and I had assumed skimming the surface of who she was would be enough. I was wrong.

Guilt waged its war within me, and I hugged my knees to my chest.

Not now, I've held it together up until this point. I can't lose hold of what I've worked so hard to maintain.

I slunk to the floor, squeezing my eyes shut. This was not how I intended my life to go. If I had just stayed put and not tried to be a hero in the eyes of our chief, I wouldn't be here. I'd be back at the manor with Silas, tending to the gardens and plucking fruit straight from the vine. There were so many beings and little, ordinary, everyday things that I missed—washing my hair, changing my clothes, sitting on the porch, taking in the sunset on hot summer days, waiting for dark. The fireflies would light up the earth, their glow coinciding with the green and gold swirls that flowed like an endless river through the valleys and over the rolling hills. I wanted to be a good sister to Nox and encourage him to follow his path, not the one chosen for him.

I missed the call of the moon, the euphoric sensation of its iridescent light traveling through my skin and into my core. My species was unknown to me, but because my power was lunar manipulation, I was immediately accepted into the Fangs of the Fallen clan. Werewolves valued brute strength, and I was one of the lucky few who did not need tribal markings to show my worth.

My eyes slowly drifted shut; the last object in my vision was a head of bleached hair.

Now shrouded in darkness, I twisted and turned while fumbling through an empty void.

"Hello?" I called out, my voice unnaturally small. This was unlike any ordinary dream. The air here was pungent, and the scent of citrus mingled with the salty air, wafting through the space. A wind from an unknown source tousled my hair, tickling my exposed skin. The veil over my eyes began to fade, morphing from unintelligible shapes into a crystal-clear scenery, and I stood on top of a familiar hillside, just outside the vineyards.

The kingdom of Alun's vibrant landscape was living and breathing in front of me, even the *Ligação Mágica* gently glided across the blades of grass, moving ever so slightly as I took a step forward. It's real, I'm home. Too scared to question how, my heart began to throb; a heavy weight lifted from my soul as I raced down the embankment and toward the manor. My feet flew across the untouched earth, and I felt nature welcome me back to my homeland with each step I pressed into her soil.

A figure abruptly materialized a few paces ahead, causing me to trip and fumble to the ground.

"Who's there?" I tensed, squinting at the foreign woman. Her satin mane was the color of night, draped over her narrow shoulders.

She cocked her head to the side, her nose scrunching up as she squinted into the fading light. The sun was beginning to set behind her, the orange glow illuminating her outline.

"...Tabitha?" she probed, my eyes going wide at the sound of my name on her lips.

"You...look like Ornella." My heart stuttered as the woman's features came into view. Her face was heart-shaped, with rounded lips, and skin as pale as the moon's; it was the perfect contrast to her raven hair. They both had the same frame and structure, just painted differently. "Sayah!" I exclaimed, finding myself on my feet. "But how are you here, how am I here?" My mind instantly backtracked, and the memories of her synchronizing with me several moons ago surfaced. The elven woman had visited me as I slept because Nox had connected us through the *Escudo das Almas* spell, implanting a fake memory to lead those spying on her mind astray.

I soaked in this bewildered woman's presence. She was Ornella's twin, and the beginning of the end, according to our captors, and in my opinion, possibly our savior. Maybe she was both.

Glancing around, I looked to see if there was anyone nearby whom I recognized. And that was when it dawned on me; there was no one, not a single soul, in this space.

Somehow, I had synced with Sayah after drifting to sleep.

I lurched for her hands, taking them in mine. An odd sensation poured into me the instant we touched, and our realities collided; it was euphoric and exhilarating. I experienced a taste of her soul, made up of memories dipped in a vibrancy of emotions. The pain of her experiences were as sharp as a knife, carving their mark on my tendrils of light. This was who she was: a vast collection of lives reincarnated, haunted by the bite of death's vengeance.

Sayah's eyes widened, and I knew that she had sensed the essence of me; I wondered what part of my soul would leave a stain on her existence because that was ultimately what occurred when you come into contact with another. An impression of you was left behind, assisting in the molding of their soul, with or without their consent.

And as *Marked Ones,* we were able to experience this phenomenon firsthand.

"You mustn't come, Sayah. You cannot go inside Mount Auberon." I squeezed her hands, pleading. "That's precisely what Bakunax wants. He needs you to break free of his confinement. I'm not sure how or why, but this much I have picked up on."

She immediately backed away as if my words had sunk their teeth into her.

"Ornella needs me. Everyone who is being held captive needs me. You need me." Her lip quivered, her grey eyes sharp with conviction. "I cannot abandon those I love, Tabitha. I am the reason Ornella was taken in the first place!" Sayah's voice rose several octaves. "I am coming, so is Nox. And Silas."

My lips opened and closed, and I was at a loss for words. Silas was coming.

"Silas?" His name was a faint whisper on my lips as my heart nearly leaped from my chest. She nodded, confirming my fears. "No!" I stumbled forward, my knees landing on the soft grass as I pulled on the hem of her pants. "Do not bring him to Adara, please! He could be killed or worse, turned into a *Thereon*! No one should come, especially not you!"

"Then what would you have us do?" Her words cut through mine, their truth seeping into my ears like poison. "If we do not go, you will die. And it will be a long, slow, and painful death. You will wither away in your prison, like a bird trapped in its cage."

The silence that followed seemed to stretch far beyond the vineyards and manor.

Sayah then took my hand and helped me up to my feet. "We have not abandoned you, Tabitha. Your family has not abandoned you."

Tears began to cascade down my cheeks as my body shook. She knew what I needed her to say, what my heart was yearning to hear. I thought of Ornella, currently in her prison, who was coming undone at the seams. I peered into Sayah's eyes, and her calm resolution was unwavering. They were a yin and yang, two opposite types of energy that complemented each other.

If I wanted to help my friend, I would have to place my trust in her twin.

"You have a plan, right? There are hundreds of *Thereon*. Multiple *Breeders* in Bakunax's army." I raised a brow, eyeing this peculiar elven girl. There was something in the way her demeanor almost challenged my own that made me smile. I dusted off the dirt on my knees out of habit, and a surge of grief overcame me in my realization.

I was not presently in Alun; I was not home in my kingdom. The dirt on my knees would vanish, the flowers and vibrant nature, the smell of the ocean and fruit would dissipate, as I was still inside Mount Auberon. My consciousness had simply linked to Sayah's, traveling to her current location.

"We have a concept of one, sure." She smiled a toothy grin, pulling me out of my thoughts, and I barked an awkward laugh.

"Wow. I haven't laughed in a long time." I rubbed my throat, taken by surprise. "I didn't know I had any joy left in me."

Sayah scratched her head as her forehead creased.

"You know, I think someone said something to me about happiness once. That it's something you create, and no one or anything can take it from you." Her hands were in mine once more, and her wide grey eyes glistened in the dim light. "Tell Ornella I said that, okay? Tell her life will find a way; hope can be reborn."

"I'll tell her. Thank you, Sayah. For not listening to me." The world around me started to haze, and I panicked. I studied every feature of Sayah's face, the way her eyes creased as she smiled. Her *Gavinhas* were onyx, with ripples of iridescent color refracting against the light. My soul bled into the illusion, seeping into the soil, the wind, the call of nature in search of my physical form. I let it pull me, though every fiber of my being fought to stay firm in the grassy hillside.

"That's something I'm terrific at. Not listening," she called out, her laughter following me like a chorus of bells, the bubbles of notes resonating with me as I floated back to the place that was the bane of my existence. That melody alone was a palpable reminder that the *Marked Ones* had not been forgotten, and a war was brewing inside the five kingdoms of Aksel.

This much I was certain.

Chapter Twenty-Two

Sovereign hands extended toward the heavens, soaked in sin,

Their palms stained crimson from the blood of their brethren,

Grasping at the fumes of what could have been deemed as forgiveness,

Mortality dissipates with their mind's eye twisted in corruption,

Blinded by greed, the five pillars fall from grace due to the *Creator's* whim,

For the monarch's focus never strayed from the divine power held hostage

over their heads,

The kingdom's sorrow and retribution tainted the royal's descent into the

eternal abyss.

PART TWO

Chapter Twenty-Three

Sayah

Adrenaline pumped through my veins as we ran into the hills, leaving the vineyards behind. My vision was enhanced from the dreamlike state I experienced moments before, when my tendrils of light blended into my line of sight, seeping back into reality from my subconscious. Nox and Silas had vanished, and in their place stood a woman with dark skin, strawberry blonde curls, and piercing blue eyes, looking dazed several feet away. Tabitha had miraculously synchronized with me, despite being outside of the range of the *Ligação Mágica*. She warned me of Bakunax, declaring it a mistake for me and the others to come to the *Marked Ones'* rescue.

The lingering feelings of happiness had all but dissipated as the reality of our situation truly set in. We were being hunted by not only *Breeders*, but those who we once considered our companions. Now the only beings we could trust were those in our inner circle; everyone else was a threat to our plans and survival.

Shuffling through the night, my throat bobbed with emotion. My desperation was coming to a peak; I would soon boil over and unravel at the seams. I shook my head, fighting off the tears. Tabitha and my sister deserved better than this mediocre rescue, and I could not let them doubt our abilities. Because the truth was, I would come to their aid, regardless of who my foe was and what dangers lay ahead.

And this was because I took sole responsibility for Ornella's capture. If I had remembered to guard her tendrils of light from the elven army using the *Escudo das Almas* spell, the elders and priests would not have had the ability to locate us through the magic.

Nox threw his arm out, catching me mid-run. Before I could speak, he placed his index finger firmly over my lips as he listened. The only noise that came to me was the pounding of my own heart in my ears, my chest rising and falling as I begged for more air. I did my best to be still, to be quiet. But I was too unbearably loud, every sound that came from me was like me blaring to those who wanted me captured that I was right here and for the taking. The sound of a twig snapping to the left sent a chill of dread throughout my body. I closed my eyes momentarily in defeat, as Nox and Silas began to growl on either side of me.

My time with Tabitha was fleeting; in the blink of an eye, and as I refocused on the present, I was now staring into the eyes of several of Nox's clan members.

Three massive warriors crouched in a defensive position, their pupils contracting in the fading light. The men's bare chests displayed their tribal markings; the swirls of enchanted ink glowed beneath the moon's presence.

My breath trembled as adrenaline flowed through my limbs, sweat lining my brow. Nox and Silas were flanked on either side of me, fangs protruding and their claws fully extended. The scenery did not match the occasion; the remnants of the orange and pink light faded into the night as the stars infiltrated nature's vast canvas around the division unfolding. There was discord among the clan members, and it was ultimately my fault. The air between us was electric; the land's magic reverberated around us under the pressure.

"Let us through, Ezra." Nox barked the command at the man standing in the middle of their pack. "This isn't a fight you want to have, not tonight under this moon."

Everyone's focus shifted to the full moon hanging low in the evening sky. I nearly audibly gasped, now seeing their glowing markings in a new light. Tonight was the night the tides could shift among the clan members; strength could be redistributed. I was unsure if they were here to ensure my retrieval or if the clan members were determined to challenge Nox for his birthright. The werewolf in the clan with the most tribal markings earned underneath a full moon was deemed worthy enough to challenge the original family members for the title of chief. From the sinister looks on the warriors' faces, I was positive they intended to accomplish both tasks.

"We take orders from Chief Phoenix, not you," he growled, his aura flashing around his figure, burning bright with energy. "He has instructed us to prevent the *Marked One* from leaving, saying she is a necessity to the betterment of The Fangs of the Fallen. You, however, are free to do as you please. And if I end up earning your markings tonight, it'll only benefit me." Ezra signaled with his fingers to the two men flanking his sides, and then they were gone, vanishing from my sight.

Silas, without hesitation, lurched toward me, throwing his hand up in the air; our eyes met for a brief instant, and an unwavering conviction reflected inside his golden irises. "*Escureo!*" the spell rang out into the clearing, and the green and gold swirls of magic snapped forward in my direction. A cloak made of the earth and sky blanketed my features; I was now invisible. He then positioned himself in front of me, speaking low. "Do not utter a sound, Sayah; make your way to the beach when you find an opening; Nox and I will meet you there."

"You used magic!" I hissed under my breath at Silas, but not before glancing over at Nox. Even fully clothed in the same black uniform as I, his tribal markings snaked their way up his neck, traveling down his arms, extending to his fingers—their glow pulsed in the moonlight, a concrete representation of power. "I can use my power to—"

"No, you will not." Silas ended my thought, shifting his body at the sound of a twig snapping in the dark to my left. "This fight involves multiple kingdoms, and they will view your use of power as a moment of weakness. The battle we are currently in is a game of strategy. Promise me, Sayah, you will stay quiet. Do not use your gift. Go to Obsydora and the other dragons; they are aware of the situation and are waiting."

A figure leapt in our direction from the shadows, cutting our conversation short. A growl ripped from Silas' throat as he collided with the werewolf who came at him full force. I jumped and tumbled in the grass, narrowly missing the collision. The two other clan members saw the opportunity to strike, lunging at Nox.

He roared, meeting their attack with intensity. This was nothing like the training exercises I had grown accustomed to watching. Their claws were fully extended, slashing at one another with the intent to eviscerate the opponent. I was frozen in place, unable to find an opening between the animalistic rage that encompassed me. Howls of pain echoed into the vineyard, and it was none other than a symphony of chaos as the sounds of flesh-tearing and bone-breaking were illuminated by the full moon.

It was now or never. I had to time it just right.

I forced my body to move, my legs and arms unnaturally heavy. Squinting past the blurs of movement, I focused solely on my destination—*the beach.* Deciding not to leave room for hesitation, I sprinted into the fray with the hope that I could somehow avoid detection and make it through the barrier of swings and punches.

As I approached the disorder, I glanced at the ripples of the *Ligação Mágica,* the magic picking up tempo as the battle progressed. A foot away from the men, I leapt into the air, pushing myself in between two figures, and snapped my fingers.

"Liguero!" I shouted midair, and a wave of green and gold tugged in my direction the instant the words were formed. My momentum shifted, and a ray of hope strummed my heart as a tingling sensation spread throughout my limbs.

But that feeling was crushed as I was hit with a solid force. A fist had penetrated my core, knocking the wind out of me, and the impact sent me colliding with the earth. My head struck the ground as I rolled, and a searing pain emanated from my skull.

"Sayah!" I heard a stifled yell to the left of me. A shadow then loomed overhead, and something wet fell onto my face. I instinctively wiped it off, inspecting my hand. It was dark and smelled of iron; it was blood.

My vision blurred, but I could sense the hostility in his aura and in the way his body shook with aggression. His yellow irises were pronounced in the momentary stillness, and a feeling of dread overtook me. All color drained from my skin; the spell that blended me into nature had vanished the second he discovered my location. The warrior within him was hidden beneath the overflowing rage, consumed by his desire for victory. He was beyond reasoning.

I felt two hands wrap around my neck, crushing my windpipe. Dazed, I tore at his grip, feverishly fighting against his strength as spots of black pulsed inside my vision.

"The chief didn't specify the condition of the *Marked One*, only that she needed to be alive." The unfamiliar voice sneered as my attempts to free myself from his grasp slowed. My consciousness was waning, and I felt my body give up before my soul. My shoulders slacked, and my head lulled to the side.

Another roar pierced the air as I found myself tumbling once more across the grass, followed by several thuds. I gasped, my hands assessing my throat as I struggled to breathe. I clenched my jaw, my eyes shut tight as my head pulsed in pain, accompanied by a ringing in my ears. I then felt someone's touch, and I winced in anticipation.

"It's me," Nox murmured, his voice shaking with several different emotions. His presence immediately put me at ease, and I felt the weight of the event begin to rise off my chest and into the stars. He cradled me in his arms, gently placing his fingertips on my neck to gauge the damage. "We need to get moving before Alizeh sends another troop in to recover you."

I mouthed the words "*Where's Silas?*" as I fought to raise my head and look for my friend.

Nox nodded his head to the right, angling me so that I could see.

Silas was standing at the top of the hill with two men at his feet. His face was tilted to the sky as he basked in the moonlight. The look of peace was etched across his features, even as he was covered in lacerations and blood pooled at his feet.

Alarmed, I fought against my aching bones and sat up using only willpower. "Will he be okay? What happened?" I croaked, my voice scraping against the back of my throat.

"He did it." Nox's voice was low, full of admiration. "He won his first fight."

My eyes went wide with shock as I continued to stare at Silas. It was as if I were seeing him in a new light. He had never been one for war, nor had he the urge to fight others in pursuit of power. His strength came from his mind, from his love for the beings he surrounded himself with.

An eerie feeling pulled at my core as goosebumps traveled up and down my spine.

"Take me to him, Nox," I whimpered, fighting back tears.

There was something I must tell him, while the wounds were still fresh, and the memory of this important event was still forming in his mind.

We began to move. Nox held me tight to his chest as we closed the distance between us and Silas. Upon closer inspection, the wounds inflicted on him were gruesome. The gashes in his skin were deep, and some of his skin hung from the bone. He would have many new scars to match the original he wore across his left eye.

"How?" I whispered, fighting back the lump forming in my throat. "How did you do it?"

Silas acknowledged us, looking away from the night sky. His brows knit together as he considered. "For the first time in my life, I had a reason to fight—a friend to protect."

My hands tightened into fists as I fought the overwhelming guilt plaguing my heart. "I am not worth the injuries, Silas. And don't tell me it's because I am a *Marked One,* a vital piece in another one of your schemes. This kind of sacrifice should have been made for Tabitha, not me." I choked back a sob as his aura flickered in and out of visibility. His tendrils of light wavered, their essence growing cold.

I knew it; his wounds were fatal.

He chuckled softly, leaning in to meet my gaze. Through all of the wounds and scars, all I could see was his bright soul shining through his almond-colored eyes. He was like the sun, a warmth I never knew I needed until his presence had gently trickled into my life. I did not want to lose him; not now, not ever.

"My love for you is no less than what I have for my partner. My heart would collapse at the thought of losing you as a friend. I cherish you, wholeheartedly," Silas whispered, a contented smile pulling at the corners of his mouth.

"You were always strong, Silas. Always have been. You never needed tribal markings or the moon's blessing to prove your worth, regardless of what your species thinks. What they believe is *wrong*." My body was wracked with rage as I uncontrollably sobbed. *I can't lose him, not now. Tabitha and Silas were so close to being reunited; I had felt the strength of their bond the instant I had synchronized with her soul. They yearned for one another with such passion that each day felt like an eternity in their eyes.*

"Sayah, no one is being sacrificed, not tonight at least. It is a full moon and Silas won; there's no need to cry." Nox nuzzled his face into my hair, kissing the crown of my head. "Watch as the moon gives her blessing."

The few sparse clouds drifted out of the moon's path, making way for her incandescent touch to absorb Silas' figure. He was a white light, shining brighter than the stars. The moonlight's healing kiss made his skin new. Just then, the two men who lay at his feet started to moan, and the swirls of black ink disappeared from their crumpled figures. My friend gasped, and markings appeared along his skin, snaking their way along his arms and upper chest. They reminded me of music notes, dancing across sheet paper to create a beautiful new song.

Silas' aura and *Gavinhas* were fully restored, and there was no sign of the pain he had endured. The only scar remaining was the one across his eye and brow, the one Nox had given him when they were in their adolescence.

They grinned at each other briefly, until their ears both twitched and their attention snapped in the direction of the manor.

"Alizeh's army is gearing up to come say hello. Let's see if we can beat them to the shoreline before we are forced to make small talk." Nox's gaze lingered on my face, his thoughts unreadable. "Sayah had the right idea earlier; we should give it another go."

I heard the snap of their fingers followed by their harmonized *"Liguero"* as they sprinted to where the rest of the crew would be waiting, along with our ill-tempered fire-breathing friends. Nox did his best to shield me from the wind as he bounded over the hills and terrain, with my face pressed into his chest. My head and body began to ache as the adrenaline from earlier waned.

As I squeezed my eyes shut, the memory of Ornella, *Mãe*, and me on the day of our rite-of-passage flashed across my mind. The flower petals that cascaded to the earth were vibrant as we walked beneath the Woodlands archway, announcing our departure with the rest of the village. My sister's melodious laugh accompanied the birds' chirping as we bounded through the forest together, approaching the *Videira*. My heart ached for the former me, the one who was oblivious to the dangers that lay ahead. I gripped his shirt, clinging to him as if he were the only thing holding me together in that instant, the thread binding me to reality.

In no time at all, I heard the lapping of waves, the sounds of muted voices, and the smell of salt mixed with smoke.

"Elven girl," Enid called to me from several paces away. The sun had set entirely, leaving us in the wake of night. At the sound of her voice, I immediately relaxed. Her calming spirit, along with the ocean's rhythmic dance on the shoreline, brought me a sense of peace in the middle of our storm.

"Why does she look like one of the dragons chewed her up and spit her out?" Kazumi accused sharply, the pesky buzz of her wings near my head was surprisingly only half as annoying as usual.

I half opened one eye, peaking at the feisty fairy.

"Some of Nox's clan got a go at her. And unfortunately, the full moon only heals werewolves after a match has been won." I twisted to look at Nox at this bit of information, my gaze studying his face and arms with intent. The scrapes and bruising had disappeared as if they had never existed.

"And what of your arm?!" I scrambled to get out of his hold, curious to see if the moon had healed his scarring from when he saved my life from being ensnared by the ancient magic on The Isles of Cadogan. Nox was adamant that the scars were his badge of honor for saving my life, and he loved them more than all of his tribal markings. However, the remorse weighed heavily on my heart, and it was a moment that someone could easily forget. *It was my hot head and impatience that led to his scarring.* The second my boots hit the sand, I turned and grabbed his right wrist to investigate. My heart dropped at the sight of the white imprints that resembled flames that encompassed the entirety of his forearm. "They're still here."

The disappointment trickled into my tone as Nox lifted my chin with his finger to meet his stare. "The moon only heals wounds that were inflicted during the current match against another werewolf. This is the way it has always been." He then nodded to Silas, standing beside him. "It's too bad that scar across your eye didn't heal, it would save me a lot of guilt."

His friend snickered, shaking his head. "I'm most grateful to have something to hold over you for the rest of your life, then." Silas retorted as he scanned the beach and the landscape behind us, his ears twitching. "We do not have long until Alizeh's army is upon us."

"I'll take a look at Sayah's bruising when we've reached the safety of the clouds." The ogress added, as she tossed a leather pack to Silas and me. "Even I can hear the sounds of their approach. If we're leaving Alun, now's the time, lads." She pointedly looked at Nox, waiting for his reply.

It was true. The sound of hundreds of feet striking the earth could be heard even at this distance, sending shivers down my spine. Their march to victory reverberated throughout nature like the rhythmic beating of a drum, the thumping of numerous hearts in unison headed our way.

"After you, milady." Nox bowed, holding out his hand to Enid. She paused, looking at him as if he were the biggest fool she had ever met.

"Naturally," Enid retorted, turning on her heel. And to my surprise, she and the others headed straight into the sea, the water immediately reaching their waists. Nox was the only one who stayed behind, waiting to see how I would proceed.

"In the water?" I raised my brows, looking at the man incredulously. "I'm not a strong swimmer."

"I won't let you sink to the ocean floor, my jewel. I promise." Nox winked before looking back over his shoulder. "But if you don't start moving, I'll be forced to carry you in."

Before I thought better of it, I turned to see what he was looking at. My heart nearly leapt out of my chest as I saw hundreds of figures outlined in the moonlight now in view. The soldiers' features weren't yet visible, nor were the whites of their eyes. *We still had time, barely.*

"You do not have to ask me twice." I awkwardly sprinted across the sand, my boots kicking up sand until I hit the water. The ocean water was lukewarm from the previous sweltering day. Nox was at my side, ready to assist me if necessary. His hands hovered at my waist, and the look of worry was etched into his brow. "It's as if you expect me to fall."

"I do suspect that you may fall. But I also expect you to be able to climb onto a dragon while half-submerged in water, so."

I bit the inside of my cheek, my face burning. "I can hold my own, you know. I've been training with Caelan for an entire lunation."

"Oh, just like you held your own back there just now?" His fingers grazed my neck, and I flinched. "If Silas weren't there, that man would've seen his last sunset."

We had caught up to the others, who were chest deep in the water—all except Kazumi, who hovered over Enid's head.

"Where's Brom?" I asked, suddenly aware of his absence.

"He was sent to retrieve our scaly friends, along with an unwanted guest." Nox's voice was tight, and if it weren't for the salt water threatening to splash in my eyes, I would've shown more concern.

"What do we do now?" The panic was rising in my chest, and I twisted away from the open sea to be greeted by hundreds of elven warriors stepping over the threshold of where the grass meets the sand. Their glare was piercing as they withdrew their swords, and from the blazing determination etched in their movements, I knew this would not be the same as when they confronted me on the beach in Erebus.

The kingdom of Alizeh had no intention of letting me walk away free. I was a prisoner under their watchful eye, a valuable asset. They did not view me as an individual, as someone who had desires, dreams of their own.

And it was in this fleeting moment that something snapped within me. The hesitation in my motives shattered, and I was filled with a surge of resolve, its electricity coursing through my fingertips.

I would answer my doubt by tearing down my fears in one blow, and as the wind whipped my hair, the salt burned my eyes; this new conviction was stronger than any other I had felt. *This is what Mãe had been trying to teach me from infancy; it was in this instance that her love and compassion, which were different from what our culture valued as imperative, suddenly made sense.*

I couldn't force anyone to accept me; it was imperative to the survival of my autonomy that I defend myself and those whom I hold close to my heart.

The stream of power deep inside my core began spilling out, flowing into the ocean as it extended to the shoreline.

I choose to protect my inner peace over the five kingdoms, regardless of the consequences.

Chapter Twenty-Four

Nox

"We do not have to do anything," I replied. Relief flooded me as my focus lingered on the clouds above. There were several massive shadows concealed in the billowy white fumes. Sayah was at my side in the shallow waters, and I perceived the slight change of intensity inside her stormy eyes. She could not help that her emotions were so easily read, and her very essence bewitched me. Her movements reminded me of a watercolor painting; the expressions cast upon her face were a glorious thing to behold, even in the darkest of moments. She was art itself, and I was mystified that the *Creator* let me linger in her presence.

A loud bellow from across the waters pulled me from her spell, and I twisted to see Brom standing on top of the sunset-colored dragon called Terragorn, the eldest and by far most massive in his horde. His body was just above the surface level; his wings tucked in as he swam with precision honed in on our location. Another figure moved into view from behind my giant ogre friend, and I audibly sighed.

Caelan was here.

My attention flickered to Sayah, who had not noticed the several dragons that now approached us from behind. Obsydora and the pesky jade dragon flanked Terragorn's sides. She was zeroed in on the elves, the species she identified as her own; her way of life had been structured around their beliefs and culture. This scenario reminded me of when we were in Erebus, except the look in Sayah's eyes had been different. There was an unsettling calm that lingered in them presently, her shoulders squared as if she were prepared to fight. The bruises on her neck said otherwise.

Silas and Enid were a few paces in front of me, and they braced themselves from the ripples of waves originating from Terragorn as he reached his destination, unfolding his left wing and creating a ramp for my friends to climb aboard.

"Break my wing and I'll break your bones," he thundered, his warning rippling in all directions.

"That is the last thing we want to happen, orange dragon," Enid snapped back, her ponytail swinging wildly back and forth as she moved up his appendage and between his shoulder blades in a mere few seconds. "We need you to be able to fly."

Terragorn snorted, his throat clicking as he spoke something unrecognizable in his species' dialect.

"Help me up," Silas shouted to the ogress, and she snatched his wrist, pulling him up the rest of the way.

"I figured you didn't need help, wolf boy." She nodded her head to his freshly added markings, the inky swirls so new they glimmered in the moonlight. "With your newfound strength, you could climb up his wings with ease."

"Enid. I wasn't worried about the climb; I was worried about Terragorn breaking my bones. I haven't tested my strength yet; I'm not sure of what I'm capable of," Silas said with a sprinkle of amusement, though it vanished instantly as the elves closed in on the shoreline.

I placed a hand on Sayah's middle back, steadying her as the ocean waves grew in strength. They were nearly breaking over her head, as our figures were naturally pulled away from land and out to open sea. "Let's get you out of the water; it can't feel good to have your clothes soaking wet."

"Everyone's clothes are wet, Nox," Sayah answered, her voice low and controlled. "I need to make sure they do not follow and track our location."

This is precisely what I was trying to avoid. She was not to use her powers unless the situation was dire, and she was already wounded. These ignorant blowhards needed to do themselves a favor and not keep picking fights with a Marked One *who can drain their energy and life source as we know it.*

"There's no need," I kept my voice calm, and eyed the sapphire dragon that swam straight for Sayah. Her yellow eyes blinked several times; the catlike pupils dilating in the dark. "Obsydora is here to give you a lift." Before she had time to process my words, I scooped her out of the water and tossed her out of the ocean. Sayah yelped, and her scaly friend caught her mid-air on her back.

Good. Now she can't do something she will regret. I turned to the army of men and women dressed in various shades of green, their camouflage more suited for the dense forests of Alizeh. Our kingdom was more fitting, however, for their attire than when we first came face to face with the elves back in the icy kingdom of Erebus. Back then, the fear in their eyes was prominent. Now they stood at the shoreline like statues, unmoving. *Wait, something is off.*

I waded through the choppy sea, approaching their stone-like figures. In the moonlight, shadows were cast about their faces, and it was as if they were paused in a moment of time, their souls stuck between the edge of life and death. It wasn't only the moon that made their complexions pale, but also the dark circles formed underneath their eyes. I focused my vision on each soldier's silhouette; their pulses thrummed in my ears. My heart dropped into the pit of my stomach, and it took all the control I possessed not to turn to look Sayah in the eye.

They had been drained of most of their energy, without anyone noticing. In the blink of an eye, their *Gavinhas* were nearly nonexistent; the soldiers' auras fading in and out. Their energy and light had been sucked dry, and they had paused in midmotion as they approached Sayah with their swords drawn and faces full of rage.

Without giving myself the moment to doubt, I turned on my heel, facing the woman who had the power to drain the life out of every living creature surrounding her. Obsydora seemed to read my thoughts, as her tongue flicked back and forth, revealing her protruding canines.

"Come on before I change my mind," she hissed, serpentine eyes narrowed.

I grunted, slipping on her scales as I fought to make my way to where Sayah rested on her back. "You're not making this any easier, you know," I quipped, raising a brow. *Dragons have such prickly demeanors.*

Sayah sat cross-legged, waiting for me to join her at her side.

"What's with that look?" She squinted, studying my expression, partially hidden by the shadows of night.

She noticed. I joined her there, cupping her face in my hands, examining her lips as if all the answers lay waiting there.

"Why did you do it?" I questioned, shoving down whatever emotion was brewing beneath the surface.

Obsydora began to flap her wings, still half submerged in the water. I shielded Sayah's face, cradling her body against mine as I found a better position to sit in. The moon's light filtered in across the water, creating a spotlight on the elven army as Obsydora and the others rose out of the water and into the air.

Sayah twisted away from me, looking down on Alizeh's defense. She murmured under her breath, her demeanor oddly still as the wind lashed about around our figures.

"What did you say?"

"I've decided to stop fighting against my instincts." Sayah glanced at me, and I saw nothing but a fierce determination in her grey irises. "Those who are important to me come first; I'm tired of fighting a battle of power I have no desire to be a part of, for beings I do not care for."

I weighed the pros and cons of what she had just done, but I knew that I would follow her down the same path, even if it led to the darkest abyss. She had drained almost all life and energy from those she opposed without so much as a blink of an eye. The soldiers' figures were now but a tiny mark on the edge of the beach, and the last of their energy depleted as their bodies crumpled to the sand below.

Chapter Twenty-Five

Tabitha

When I came to, the air was humid; the ground beneath me was cold and uneven. A repetitive clanking reverberated up the cavern walls, piercing whatever thoughts that lingered into two. I sat up, my body groaning in protest. I had never left the kingdom of Adara, and my eyes hadn't witnessed the sunlight in many moons. But it was as if I was in my cage for the first time, and my vision struggled to adjust to the dim light. A figure stirred in the prison adjacent to mine, and I blinked several times. Ornella's withered body lay in a crumpled heap, and she fought to pull herself up onto her elbows. It was as if I were witnessing one's inner demons slowly begin to possess their external appearance; her once pure white waves were dull and matted, and bruises littered her skin, the shackles around her wrists just as heavy as the weight of the world sitting on her sagging shoulders. But the most vital evidence to this claim was found residing in her emerald eyes; hope and fear no longer lingered there, only pain. She was morphing into the being in her nightmares.

"Ornella," I whispered, trying to grab her attention without alerting several of the *Thereon* that lingered by in the cavern's labyrinth of connecting pathways. "I spoke to your sister—I synchronized with Sayah." My words came out rushed, as I was unable to hide my excitement. "She's on her way here, and she says she would never abandon you."

Her head snapped in my direction, the news sparking energy back into her movements.

"You...synchronized with Sayah?" She annunciated each syllable, carefully flipping over the words in her mind. "That can't be possible; it must've been a dream. I'm her twin, her sister, and I can't manage to make contact. We're too far from the *Ligação Mágica*; there's no way you were able to without having built a connection with her first."

I shook my head in earnest. "I think...this wasn't the first time. We both recognized each other immediately." I then scooted to the side of my cage, my hands gripping the iron bars. "But that is not the point. They are on their way to save us; I'll get to see Silas." My grip released from the bars, and I sat back in disbelief at the feeling of hope surging through me.

Silas will be before me; in the flesh; no longer a figment of my imagination.

Just the thought had my heart yearning for him once again. I hadn't dared to let myself think of the possibility until this very moment. I missed the depth in his stare, the way he would whisper sweet nothing in my ear as we lay in the hammock beneath the stars.

As I was caught inside my own illusions, Ornella had begun to pace back and forth. The scraping of metal as the chains dragged across the floor brought me back to the present. I did not interrupt her thoughts; the crazed look in her eyes told me she was on the verge of snapping. Her hair hung limply over her face; her back was hunched as she mumbled, lost in thought. Finally, she whipped her head in my direction, and her features no longer possessed those of a normal being. They were demented; her irises dilated from the lack of sleep and emotional turmoil.

"Maybe it will be easier for me, now that you've made contact with Sayah." Her speech was slurred, her thoughts a scrambled mess. "I am going to try again. I will synchronize with her before she arrives; I know I can do it. She's *my* sister, after all." She sat back down with her legs crossed and back erect, facing away and toward the inner caverns.

My shoulders slumped, and I murmured in her direction, knowing that my worry would fall on deaf ears, "Don't push yourself too hard, Ornella."

But it was far too late for that, as she was long beyond the point of reason.

Chapter Twenty-Six

Ornella

*H*ow, and why? That was the question that I found myself repeating over and over, in the days that were to come. *How was Tabitha able to connect with Sayah's wavelengths without trying? And why was it so diffi-cult for me?* None of it made sense. Nothing made sense to me anymore. Not even the chaos that resided here in Mount Auberon. The *Thereon* had started a new pattern of digging farther into the rock beds, attacking the walls in their random fits of terror. Some of the soulless beasts bashed their heads against the rock, the repetitive clanking ringing in my ears. They lusted after the *Breeders'* blood, or more precisely, Bakunax's blood. He began to hold the black liquid over their heads as if it were a consolation prize, and the *Thereon* who pleased him most that day would win. But I knew what he was up to, as he slithered up and down inside the mountain that was his cage. Bakunax was preparing for my sister's arrival, as she was somehow the key to his being freed from the ancient spell that had held him hostage for thousands of lunations. That old and powerful magic was the only thing keeping him and his army from completely descending on the other four kingdoms.

I cast a glance at Tabitha, who kept herself busy by watching the *Breeders* and their movements. The used-to-be dragons had moved up from the depths of the caves, and in return, they dragged hordes of gold and jewels up and into the forefront with them. Every so often, the monstrosities would snack on the *Thereon,* their cries bleeding into my ears and searing my thoughts. The smell of decaying flesh would reach even the heights of our cages and cause me to heave uncontrollably.

There was a heavy weight of anxiety that lingered in the air, weighing intensely on the *Marked Ones* who still had the strength and mental fortitude. Unfortunately, I noticed the ones who had first arrived were still in their cages, and no sound was uttered from their cells. The bread that was tossed at their feet remained untouched, mold festering on its edges. I wondered if the smell of decaying flesh came from below or adjacent to me.

I shook my head, unwilling to focus on the ugly truth butting its head into my mind every once in a few moons' time—*that we will all meet an unfortunate demise.*

"Do you see that?" Tabitha had moved closer to my cage as I was lost in my thoughts. She was pointing down to the largest opening, which led to the cave's mouth. Clouds of smoke were pouring into the space, trickling past the *Thereon* that were oblivious to the fumes.

"I see it, but I don't understand what I am looking at." I squinted into the darkness, and several dark figures darted out of the smoke and along the cave walls, snaking their way between the patches of stalagmites dispersed throughout the rocky terrain.

"Are my eyes playing tricks on me, Tabitha? Or did you see—"

"Hush." Her crystal blue eyes were wide, and she gestured for me to sit down. "We do not want to bring attention to whatever is happening now. Pretend to be asleep."

I obeyed, resting my body on the iron floor with my head strategically facing the *Breeders of Thereon* and their army. It was difficult not to let the rising hope fill my chest, not to let Tabitha's excitement rattle my reality. We were still trapped in our cages, which were surrounded by a blue ancient magic, and there was no definitive way of knowing what was happening at the threshold.

Every muscle in my body was tense as I lay waiting. Waiting for something to happen, some form of a signal or sign. But in my anticipation, my bones began to ache, my eyes started to water from lack of blinking, and my heart rate slowed. The tension never alleviated from my form; I was still in the same position as when I first rested my head on the hard surface, and my eyelids began to close as I drifted off into a fitful slumber.

"Psst! Ornella, wake up!" Tabitha whisper-screamed as I groggily woke, only to find black fumes of smoke shrouding my vision. The entire space was filled with the mysterious gas, and I coughed as it burned my throat and eyes.

"My brethren have finally come to greet me, after all this time." Bakunax's voice bellowed from somewhere inside the dark cloud. "I am surprised to see you working side by side with a *Marked One*, and here I thought you hated their existence."

I paused mid-thought, mulling over his words.

What could he possibly mean by that? Dragons hate Marked Ones?

Bakunax must be lying; Fraener had said that he was the most cunning of them all. He must be trying to wedge doubt in between those who were here to rescue us.

"Do not listen to the lies he spreads!" Tabitha screamed into the void. I could make out her silhouette, and she was pressing her body against her cage, all of the hate for the vile creatures exploding out of her mouth and being made known. "Bakunax speaks only lies! As do all those who work for him! Do not listen to another word from him, Sayah!"

"*That's enough from you.*"

The cold, calculated voice snapped at Tabitha from the labyrinth of tunnels behind us. The man with the multicolored eyes, Ein, was unexpectedly there, as if he lay waiting for the most inopportune moment to show his snake-like face.

"You are officially no longer useful to me and can be disposed of accordingly," he mused, and I witnessed in horror as the black magic that clung to him reached for where the chain of her cage met the cavern ceiling. The entity writhed as it held on to the restraint, slowly ripping it from its foundation. Rocks came loose and fell with the repetitive motion. Cracks rippled throughout the cavern's ceiling; the entire heart of the mountain shook in protest.

"No!" A guttural scream erupted from my chest as I clung to the rusted iron bars.

"Ornella!" Tabitha cried out, her voice trembled with fear as it echoed from inside her enclosure, as the chains were yanked away from the limestone.

"Tabitha!" I choked on her name as the ceiling gave way, and her cage disappeared into the black fumes. "What have you done?!" I cried in dismay, gritting my teeth at Ein. My grip tightened around the iron bars, and an animalistic scream left my throat. The sound of Tabitha's prison crashing to the floor had me fall to my knees in despair. I did nothing to stop my mourning as sobs escaped from deep within my chest. *I hated him, I hated him with every ounce of my being.*

Ein approached my cage with ease, standing on the ledge of the stairway that was carved into the ancient stone.

"I rid myself of a nuisance; that's what I've done." All that was visible in the smoke was his green and gold eyes. He raised a brow, his gaze raking me over. "You haven't been taking care of yourself, it seems. And that was her whole purpose, to give you the will to live while we waited on your sister's arrival."

My mouth opened and closed as I was unable to find words.

"It is only fitting that you understand the fate I've prepared for you and your sister." He scratched his chin, his face now radiating delight. "I have gathered all the *Marked Ones* here, in search of you and your twin. You two are the only ones of use to me. The rest can die a miserable death for all I care." He shrugged his shoulders, and he picked at his teeth as if we were chatting over afternoon tea, not over my friend's grave.

"Why...why do you need us?" I questioned, my body shivering uncontrollably.

"You two have what is rightfully mine; my birthright." Through the smoke, I saw his finger pointing directly at my chest. "Those powers that flow in your veins are mine. The only reason I have yet to drain them from you and restore my gift is because Bakunax needs you to break through the barrier to infiltrate *Paraiso*, my homeland."

I sat up, in awe of his insanity. "We were born with these powers, Ein. How can they be yours when the *Creator* gifted them to my sister and me specifically?"

"Do not utter my name!" he hissed, running his hands through his white hair in frustration. "We come from the same bloodline. You, your sister, and I were born from the same mother. Etienne gave birth to me several lunations before you even existed."

"That can't be!" My chest heaved, my eyes watering in protest. I stumbled, my back pressing against the far end of the cage, as far away from the abomination in front of me. "You are not my family!"

"Oh, believe me, I am not thrilled that I am related to you either. But I have had more time to process." He sighed, clearly annoyed.

The smoke had begun to dissipate, and it was as if I were seeing this vile man for the first time. And no matter how much I wanted to deny it, the truth was blaring. His long white waves, his single emerald eye, and his pointed nose. It was as if I were staring into a mirror. A lump formed in my throat, and my shivers turned into a cold sweat. I did not recognize his gold eye or his square jawline.

"What you accuse me and Sayah of; it doesn't make sense," I muttered, inching toward him as my voice slowly climbed. "You were born *first*. First!

How could we have stolen your gift from the *Creator* if we had yet to exist?!"

"You're such an ignorant fool!" Ein growled, shaking his head. "The *Creator* only shaped gifts for the *Estrella*; the original bloodline and species. Gifts are not earned or given; they are passed down. Etienne defied me as I grew in her womb because she did not love my father. And my mother didn't love me enough to leave me with at least some form of protection. She hated me as I grew in her belly." His face was inches from the bars, the ancient blue magic cracking around his silhouette. "No; instead, she made herself an outcast and had children with a species that is lesser than. A lowly elf. It's despicable."

"Our birth mother...chose us for these powers?" I stared at my dirt-ridden fingertips, dumbfounded.

"*No.*" He tapped his foot, and his brow twitched in irritation. "She did not choose you; she chose to deny me. Whomever she gave birth to from her womb next would have received my powers, my birthright. That gift of yours? It was never yours to begin with. It was a mistake. You and your sister's existence tainted our perfect bloodline, along with the rest of these *Marked* creatures. In my eyes, you're no different from them."

Ein gestured to the *Thereon*'s blood-curdling cries, and it was only now that I noticed the chaos ensuing at the cavern's base.

The *Thereon* encompassed the hooded figures, as smoke still lingered about the space. Several of their rotting corpses were impaled on the stalagmites, the smell of their decaying flesh mixing with the flames that the *Breeders* shot out of their mouths at their opponents; they did not care if their own creations were burnt into nothing but ashes in the process. It was absolute pandemonium, and my eyes went wide with fear as my cage began to tilt, as the ceiling crumbled to the floor, the sediment falling onto several of the *Thereon.*

"You're too valuable to me; I can't let you die here." He popped the lock off my prison, just as it came unhinged from the ceiling. A scream rose in my throat, and I covered my face with my arms, bracing for impact. But my body was forced forward, not down. When I opened my eyes, I was hovering over the battle beneath me, held up by the parasitic magic attached to the man I hated most. The entire mountain was rumbling, shaking in an uproar in retaliation for the havoc taking place inside.

"What about the others? You can't leave them here, they will die!" I pleaded, desperate for him to do the same for the others that he did for me.

"They're dying, or already dead," he answered, pulling me to the ledge and pushing me into the shadows of the tunnels. "You should've learned by now, I don't like being asked to do favors, especially when there's nothing in it for me. Oh, wait, that was your sister." He barked a laugh as I lay there in a crumpled heap on the ground. Ein took his boot, kicking me hard in the side. I grunted, gasping for the air he just forced out of my lungs.

"Get up, and get moving." He hovered over me, finally within reach. Fear jolted down my spine, and it was not from the mountain crumbling to pieces around me. He violently grabbed my hair at my scalp, pulling me up from the floor. The scream that involuntarily exploded from my pain was lost in the sea of chaos. "I will leave this cave with what I traveled across The Arching Depths for."

I moved blindly, as I ambled deep into the caverns, where I had dreamt of exploring and envisioning myself finding an escape from this pit of despair.

My fingertips felt the grooves along the cold and rigid walls, slicing my palms as I left a trail of blood for unknown souls to follow.

We took a sharp left, and I felt the weight of two hands shove me from behind as I fell further into the darkness. My body caught on several hard edges as I cried out, desperate to catch myself and find my footing.

"Ungrateful brat. Make haste, or we'll end up being crushed to death." His words sliced through the shadows with venom—an added salt to my wounds.

I said nothing; I merely followed orders and quickened my pace.

We were headed out of caverns; out of this treacherous abyss. My heart danced in my chest, and despite the abuse, the cuts and bruises, I felt joy. Because what I craved most in this world was closer than I had ever imagined possible: freedom from the *Breeders of Thereon* and my prison.

The entire cave hummed with warning as I now practically skipped down the rocky terrain; the single thought that concerned me was my survival. *I refused to die without seeing the sunlight and experiencing its warmth at least one more time.* That is what I craved most in this world.

But what of Tabitha, of Sayah, and the others? This question bled into my thoughts as the descent rapidly decreased and I realized we had made it to the cavern's main entrance.

An odd sound came from my right, and Ein shouted. *"Move!"* he kicked my body across the dark cavern, just as the ceiling above us began to collapse. I hit the ground and rolled, as pain radiated from every inch of me. I was already littered with bruises, and I wouldn't be surprised if I now had broken bones.

I instinctively covered my head with my arms in a fetal position as I waited for the small avalanche of rocks to subside before moving. Right as I went to open my eyes, I felt two hands on my shoulders, and I froze.

"It's me," a familiar voice said with a gentle reassurance.

And that was all it took for me to jerk my head in her direction, tears already flowing down my cheeks. "Enid!" I scrambled up from the floor, looping my arms around her neck. I sobbed into her collarbone as she patted me on the back.

"Elven girl, now is not the time to celebrate. Not yet." She moved me to her side, placing an arm across my figure protectively. Her stance was tense, and because I had been so relieved by her unexpected presence, I had briefly forgotten that Mount Auberon was beginning to crumble.

Ein was trapped behind several boulders, his multicolored eyes narrowed as he took in the ogress's presence. But time was not on our side, and the vibrations surrounding us grew in strength. That was when I noticed movement along the cavern walls. *Thereon* were there, attacking the rock as they dug into the very infrastructure that held the mountain upright. I froze, the realization leaving my mouth agape. *They were ordered to make the mountain fall, by their Breeders—by Bakunax. He knew Sayah would come for me, and now that we were here, his plan to escape had already been set into motion.*

Bakunax would make the Mount Auberon fall.

"Where are the others?" I panicked, squinting into the darkness. All I could hear were the sounds of the ghastly beasts' screams and grunts echoing all around me.

Enid started to pull me forward, ignoring Ein. "They are with Silas; he has Tabitha." Her voice grew solemn, and my body was overtaken with emotion as I paused, shaking.

"Is she...?" I choked, my vision blurred.

"She's alive, elven girl." Her tone was rough, and her fists clenched at her sides. "She's alive, but she needs energy. She needs *you*."

I audibly sucked in a breath, looking Enid in the eyes for the first time. Her brown irises were stern, cold even. And I knew what needed to be done.

"Take me to her," I commanded, as my body moved solely from pure determination. *Tabitha needed energy, and I was willing to give every last drop of mine to keep her alive—and Enid knows this. It's why she didn't come right out and say it in the first place.*

Wordlessly, we began to move, as pebbles and debris landed their mark as they fell from the ceiling. I twisted around one last time and glanced at my captor. Ein was wedged between the boulders and the cavern wall, his eyes piercing in the dark.

"Thank you for saving me," I mouthed. I wasn't sure why I thanked him at all, because he didn't deserve it. He was cruel and should be shown no mercy. And yet, I found myself guilt-ridden because I did not try to save him in his time of need.

Ein scoffed, a grimace now plastered on his features. "I didn't save *you*. I saved what was mine that *you* stole. So, you can wipe that look of pity off your ugly mug."

My cheeks heated, and I turned away from the horrid man. I was angry with myself for believing there was some good left in him. *Why was I always a fool?*

"I hope you are buried in this pile of rubble when it's all said and done," I yelled over the sounds of the world around me collapsing. A thought then pierced my mind, feeding into the hate that had burrowed its way into my heart.

I hope he dies for taking mãe's life, and for all the other souls I know nothing about.

I hope he pays for his sins in the most painful way possible.

Chapter Twenty-Seven

Sayah

The kingdom of Adara was the epitome of what I envisioned the depths Bakunax himself had crawled out of. It was a bleak, horrid landscape. This much was evident even in the shadows cast by the fading sun. Night was approaching as the horde of dragons flew over the top of the mountain, and to my dismay, all that remained of the homes of those who once lived here were their singed foundations. The *Ligação Mágica* endlessly tremored in the presence of evil, the movements of the green and gold swirls jagged and in complete disorder. I had never witnessed the land's magic in such peril in all the moons I have lived. It was far worse than when the *Thereon* would make their appearance in the other kingdoms. This is where the origin of all sin and evil resided.

Our crew had traveled for days on end; the dragons took breaks and swam while fishing occasionally. There was an unspoken understanding that resonated in the air, as it was dense with solemnness and unease. I instinctively shook my head, trying to rid myself of such negative thoughts. My arms flexed, adrenaline pumping through my veins. *Don't fall prey to your anxieties, Sayah. You are more than ready.* Ornella and the others had waited far too long, and guilt tugged at my chest. *All that matters is that we are here now.*

I looked to those I cared for, hopeful. We were all apprehensive about what was to come, and therefore, we distracted ourselves with the usual banter and bickering. Nox seemed a bit off as of late, keeping more to himself. And if I weren't so worried about Ornella and my vital role in our schemes, I would have confronted him immediately. But my thoughts were elsewhere entirely; I was envisioning myself in combat, running through the scenarios that had been drilled into me by Caelan over and over. Silas was strapping several daggers to various parts of his body as he sat atop Terragorn. He had gone over the plan with me multiple times, and I was prepared. *He told me I was anyway, and that was enough for me to convince myself of it too.*

"You alright there, Elvin girl?" Enid poked her head out behind several dragons standing on the black soot. We had taken cover just outside of the cave's mouth behind several large boulders. "I disagree with Silas, you know. You don't have to go through with his plan."

"He said it's the most foolproof bet of everyone making it out alive. So of course I'm going through with it." I tightened the laces on my boots, checking my own gear. We all had on the identical army-grade suits, made of durable, thin black leather. It made the perfect camouflage for the landscape riddled with nothing but the shadows of the past.

"Silas thinks with logic, not feelings," Brom said from behind me, patting me on the back a little too hard, causing me to fall forward and off the small boulder I was perched on. "If you feel like this task is too big for you, let us know and we can go with another one of his crazy plans."

A flash of pink buzzed by my ear, and I fought the urge to roll my eyes. "And Brom thinks with his stomach," Kazumi spat, the feisty fairy always quick with her sharp tongue.

Brom's face flashed full of hurt, and Enid narrowed her gaze on the fairy who was hovering on my shoulder. I shooed her away with my hand, but not before she nipped at my fingers.

"Now is not the time to argue." I stood, weaving my hair back into one tight braid. "Wait, when did I become the level-headed one? Something's already amiss, and we haven't even entered the cave yet."

A shadow fell over my figure, and goosebumps traveled up my spine.

"You're ready to see Ornella again." Nox was suddenly in my ear, and a blush momentarily ran up my neck and cheek. "And I'm ready to see my sister. And so is someone else." We both glanced over at Silas, who was keeping himself busy by checking to see how everyone else was doing. *He has yearned for Tabitha for so long, and now he would finally get to see her. I would make sure of it.*

Nox then lightly pecked my forehead before heading over to the newest member of our crew. My heart always dropped into my chest whenever they interacted, and it was right to do so, because their clans paired them together after all. *I was the one who was in the middle of—whatever this was.*

All that I knew for certain was that I had feelings for Nox, and he had some feelings for me. Could I define them? Not exactly, but it was made apparent that he cared for me. And that was enough, for now.

Caelan always appeared ready for battle at a moment's notice; that was most likely because her cheekbones could slice through stone, and her muscles were nearly the size of Nox's. She marched up to me after a quick word with him, eyes narrowed.

"Think you can pull this off?" she murmured, raking over me with her gaze.

"Does anyone other than me think so? Because it seems like the answer to that is a big fat no." I met her stare and let out a large sigh. "While everyone else is fighting, I'll sneak up behind Bakunax without getting myself killed or turned into a *Thereon*, and drain his energy along with the other *Breeders*. Doesn't sound too difficult to me." I shrugged, pretending to look off into the distance. "For Ornella, for Tabitha, for all of those who have been rotting away in this cursed mountain, I can do it. I'll find the courage."

"That's the spirit." Kazumi was back, grinning with her jagged teeth inches away from my eyes. "I'm relaying the message that the dragons are now ready, so it's time to start moving."

I gulped, nodding.

Obsydora, Terragorn, and a few other dragons had snaked their way through the rocky terrain and were strategically positioned on either side of the cave's opening.

"Everyone, remember to pull your hoods up," Silas quipped, jogging next to Nox and Brom. "The goal is to get in and get out as quickly as possible. We do not want to have to fight, if we can avoid it." He then eyed me over, deep in thought. "Sayah, you are vital if things do not go according to plan. You must drain their energy before they are alerted to our presence."

"Yeah, I don't want to be eaten, or worse, turned into one of the *Breeders'* undead minions," Kazumi snapped, and I did, in fact, roll my eyes at this remark.

"You are so small they wouldn't even call you a meal," I muttered under my breath, and she hissed in response.

Nox was crouched beside me, and I studied every inch of his face. The hard lines from having to make difficult decisions from a young age, his chiseled jaw line. The way his russet eyes held a depth to them, the look of determination and resilience. I wanted to freeze time right here and take in his presence wholeheartedly.

His gaze found mine, and he rested his index finger beneath my chin, brushing his thumb over my lips. "I go in first, and you follow behind. I'll get you to the position that you need to be in, and from there, we'll improvise."

"It's the improvising that scares me," I admitted, swallowing the lump that threatened to resurface in my throat.

"You're in luck, then, my jewel, because improvising is what I'm best at." Nox winked, and the mischievous look etched into his features brought forth a smile on mine. *If we were not in such a precarious situation, I absolutely would have stuck my tongue out at him. I had a love-hate relationship with his ridiculous nickname for me.*

"*Marked One,* the horde and I will do what we can from the outside. We will not risk our souls for this endeavor." Obsydora blinked, her cat-like eyes never leaving my face. "The spell that keeps the *Breeders of Thereon* inside would forbid us from leaving the caverns of Auberon. I hope you and your comrades understand."

"I understand." The sapphire dragon's words had me sober up in an instant, and I placed a hand on her long snout. "I'll be back out here with Ornella before you have time to rest your eyes and relax. I'm similar to a hatchling in that way. A headache to take care of, but you can't help but love me anyway." She blew a puff of smoke around me as I mischievously grinned.

"Be prepared for anything, *Marked One*. Bakunax is cunning. I would not be surprised if he knew we were outside of his prison, and he lay waiting with a plan of his own." She shook her head, as if she were shaking the thought out of her mind. "When the entire tunnel fills with smoke, enter the chamber and stay within its camouflage."

A cold chill ran down my spine, and I nodded.

We crouched behind several boulders outside the threshold of the cave. I could not see this ancient spell, but I could feel its power vibrating in my bones. It hummed with an electricity the closer we stood to the cave's entrance. The dragons continuously blew funnels of smoke, which rose high inside the caverns and touched the ceiling.

When we all entered the cavern, my eyes burned from the fumes. I kept them closed, trying not to cough in the suffocating darkness. One hand trailed the limestone; the other was in Nox's as he led the way. I felt a sense of peace as I heard the shuffling of feet, knowing that my friends were still nearby. Kazumi was concealed in Enid's clothing and would reveal herself when they made it to the cages above. She was literally our key for silently breaking the locks without making so much as a peep.

Everyone had a role to play; we were all integral to the escape of the *Marked Ones*. I felt it was my responsibility to save every last soul from Bakunax's clutches as I was the last *Marked One* who had not been captured.

Nox abruptly stopped in front of me, and I ran into his back, nearly stumbling onto the ground. "What's wrong?!"

"We are almost out of the tunnel, and inside the main chamber," he whispered, so quietly that I had to strain my ears to hear over the shouts and cries up ahead. "This is where we split off into groups."

"You do not need to tell me twice," Caelan chirped, moving out from directly behind my shadow. She disappeared into the smoke, veering off out of sight. My face had momentarily paled, and I had forgotten entirely of her presence. *I wonder what she thought of Nox and me being so close.* The others dispersed, as I listened to their feet shuffling off into various directions.

"Where are the *Thereon* at, Nox?" I questioned, not actually wanting to know an answer. I tripped and stumbled over several loose rocks every few feet, and his hand was the singular reason I stayed upright.

Not paying clear enough attention to my surroundings, I suddenly walked into the back of Nox. The black fumes had not yet dissipated, and unidentifiable noises came from directly in front of us. "I think we've found them, unfortunately. Get ready Sayah."

I blinked several times, my eyes dry from the lack of moisture in the air. Growls and shrieks echoed and bounced off the walls; the desire for their *Breeder's* blood rumbling deep from their throats. *Bless the vine;* they were all piled in the corners of the chamber, and it was as if they had gone completely mad. The *Thereon* gnashed their limbs and heads into the walls of the cavern, chipping away at the foundation as rocks flew in every which direction. It wasn't until we were close that the putrid smell hit me; the smoke must have been concealing it. It reeked of rotting flesh and death, and that was when I noticed the *Thereon's* greyish skin had begun to fall off their bones. I had never witnessed such an unsettling sight. This was the consequence of the *Breeder's* puppets. No longer did they have souls; no longer did they have any wants or needs outside of what their master desired. Their *Gavinhas* were gone, and without tendrils of light to connect them to this world, they had begun to decay as the parasitic magic surrounding them kept their corpses upright. It was a far worse fate than simply dying; it was an act of blasphemy. And the soulless beasts were so consumed in their task that they did not notice us standing a few feet away.

Our options were grave. It was either we faced the *Thereon* here, or we risked going straight into the heart of the chamber and facing off with their *Breeders.*

I did not have time to blink before Nox had unleashed his razor-sharp claws, his fangs protruding as an animalistic growl ripped from his chest. He was on the offensive, and he leaped into the mass of *Thereon,* slicing at their cores and tearing into the decrepit monsters. Though he could damage their withering flesh, the black magic wound its grip on the soulless beasts tighter, weaving a path along the skeletons and melding into the corpse. The inky substance was sin personified; it sank its insidious grip into the bones of the undead, and the tortured bodies would never know peace.

One of them escaped Nox's grasp, hurling all of its weight straight at me with uncontrolled force. I dove out of the way, its figure knocking me into the center of what was now chaos. Pain radiated through my limbs, and I froze on the ground. All that was visible was the bottom half of their statures, and I recognized Brom and Enid's broad forms not too far from where I landed.

I turned to look for Nox, but it was a sea of black as the soulless beasts grew in numbers. *Bakunax has to know that we are here by now; our cover is blown. Our best chance of surviving is for me to drain him of his energy without him noticing.*

I looked for a place to hide, but still close enough to the center, where the *Breeders* would undoubtedly lie waiting. Their massive frames were too large for them to reside in the labyrinth of tunnels branching out into the outskirts of the mountain.

"My brethren have finally come to greet me, after all this time," Bakunax roared from up ahead. "I am surprised to see you working side by side with a *Marked One*, and here I thought you hated their existence."

I held my breath before shaking my head. His declaration was a glaring lie. *Dragons hate our existence? Nonsense. No, Obsydora cares for me.* And yet I glanced over my friends protecting me and back toward the exit, as a seed of doubt was planted in my heart.

"Do not listen to the lies he spreads!" Someone screamed out from the shadows. "Bakunax speaks only lies! As do all those who work for him! Do not listen to another word from him, Sayah!"

My eyes shot up to the ceiling at the mention of my name, and there she was in her prison high above the stalagmites—*Tabitha.*

And before I had time to react, the vile monsters screeched and moved with a new intensity. The threat started to close in, and as several Thereon flanked my sides, several screams of terror pierced through the air, sending a shiver down my spine. *I knew that scream; that voice was etched into my heart's memory.*

"Ornella?!" I panicked, adrenaline kicking in as I did the one thing I was told not to do—I ran straight up the center of the chamber and into the pandemonium, alone.

And I sprinted into the most enormous dragon I've ever seen, towering over my figure. He had the same parasitic magic clinging to his crimson scales, but he still had tendrils of light attached to him—only they were black like mine. His soulless eyes scrutinized every inch of me as he bared his canines and flicked his serpentine tongue.

"At last, the one I've been waiting for; the one who was born from sin—you and I are the same." His voice shook the earth beneath me, as if he spoke, thunder was born into existence from simply uttering his thoughts.

"I am nothing like you." I quivered, fear once again taking hold of me. *This is not how the plan was supposed to go; this is not how things were supposed to happen.*

"*Marked One,* you speak out of ignorance. Child, *you* know nothing. You and I are a combination of circumstances: a lack of love and an uncontrollable desire to protect what we deem as necessary. I can see this strength inside of you; the ability to cast aside those who are lesser than."

"No—you're wrong." But even as I rebuked his words, I knew there was a sliver of my soul that agreed with him. That I was capable of casting aside beings whom I thought were a threat to anyone I cherished. The faces of Alizeh's soldiers came to mind; the fear melded into their features as I drained them of their energy. "How can you know so much about me by a simple glance?"

How smart was Bakunax? Did he have the ability to synchronize and read one's memories without a connection to the magic? No, that was impossible. The Creator renounced the beast of this ability long ago. He could no longer connect to the Ligação Mágica, the green and gold swirls of tangible magic that sat in a constant state of disarray outside this very cavern.

The entire mountain rattled, and the cages perched precariously at the highest peak of the cave began to clamber to the ground.

"No! The *Marked Ones*!" I whipped my head to Bakunax, finding my courage. "Are you not going to save them? Don't you need their powers?" I searched his eyes in desperation, but found a lack of emotion that sent goosebumps down my spine.

"Those are just their corpses. They were gradually drained of their power and life source while rotting away inside their cages. It was unbeknownst to them, a slow and miserable death." His tail swished at this, creating more piles of rubble. "Do not worry, though, I kept your sister with a companion on the adjacent side of the room, so they are mostly unaffected by my methods."

"No...we are here to save them from that fate; it can't be." Distraught, I staggered back, my heart pounding in my chest.

The promise that I made to Tabitha...the promise I made to everyone. To myself. I was the reason we hadn't left for Adara for several moons...because of my lack of control over my powers and my inability to fight in combat. Even now, I was mediocre. We had only left the kingdom of Alun when we did because Alizeh forced our hand. This entire situation —the Marked Ones' deaths—was all my fault; it was all my doing.

"And because you came, *Marked One*, it has set everything into motion. Everything is falling into place." He lowered his massive head, his breath foul, death lingering between his teeth. "The cage that has held me for thousands of lunations will fall; I will be set free."

I shook my head, tears in my eyes. "This is not because of me. You will not be freed."

Bakunax's laugh was sinister as he leaned in close, his eyes reflected the heaps of gold and jewels beneath him. "The moment you took what was not yours, this was *your* doing. *You stole their souls.*"

Time itself seemed to stop, and the foundation of who I was came crashing down, and my head spun with flashes of iridescent light, and floating orbs swam around my figure.

A hand suddenly found mine in the darkness, pulling me away from Bakunax and the cave that was crumbling into pieces. And I cried, unable to look away from the monster who was the epitome of evil with his wicked grin carved into his features.

I cried because I somehow knew he was right.

Chapter Twenty-Eight

Ornella

The sun was scorching hot; it was nothing like I had envisioned. The ball of fire was not a welcomed embrace, and instead, a stranger seeping its blazing heat into my skin, screaming for repentance as it peeled off what little identity I had left. The air was too sharp, the wind feeling like a thousand knives taking aim at my figure as I sat atop Fraener as we soared above the clouds.

I unclenched my hands from my sides, the crease in my brow permanent as I glanced over at Terragorn. Silas was cradling a body close to his chest as he sat atop the dragon, his gaze never leaving her unflinching face. *Tabitha.*

She was limp, the rise and fall of her chest uneven. The descent from her cage to the floor would have killed an ordinary being, and the single reason she was alive was that she was a *Marked One*, gifted with the powers of controlling lunar energy. As the cave collapsed, Tabitha was brought out into the moonlight for the first time in many lunations, where her broken body absorbed enough energy from the moon to keep her heart beating. And I had used my powers to gift her with as much energy as I could before I was on the brink of collapse; it had been just enough to keep her tendrils of light from dissipating.

The urgency to make it to the uncharted part of the map had grown tenfold the instant she was severely injured. Not to mention the *Breeders'* and Ein's fates were unknown.. But we needed to find sanctuary, away from the four kingdoms where other species resided.

Is Sayah right, and Bakunax was now free from the ancient spell that bound him to the horrid regions of Adara? Only time would tell.

The only momentary solace I found was that I was alone with the jade dragon, who had a naturally sour attitude, and whom I had missed dearly. Clouds gradually began to disperse, and I scanned the horizon, searching. For what, I wasn't sure exactly. The ocean was bleak over The Arching Depths, the *Ligação Mágica* in disarray as the green and gold swirls swayed beneath the surface; a constant reminder of the army of *Thereon* possibly looming behind us. And not only the *Thereon*, but Ein would be leading them—that vile man. A small part of me was glad the cave fell, only because I managed to escape his capture from the falling rocks. There was no sense of security in our situation, however, as we were headed to his homeland. But it was the only place that dragons could not willingly enter through themselves, Obsydora had explained. That was why they found refuge on the Isles of Cadogan when we first ran into their legendary species. As we distanced ourselves from the chaos, we passed by the group of islands, and the mist of the border between the five kingdoms and the unknown was visible. There was a sudden shift in mood between our crew and even amongst the horde of dragons. The quiet grew in intensity, while the hatchlings moved more freely from the elders hovering in the center of their flight formation.

My focus shifted to studying Fraener's scales as I ran my fingers over their smooth yet sturdy texture. Their shape reminded me of miniature shields, and the emerald held bits and pieces of other hues, buried within their intricate design. Each scale was like a piece of a story, and when they were placed together, the sea of shapes created the beautiful creature that I knew as the short, stalky dragon that would only let *Marked Ones* ride upon his back.

I sighed, briefly placing my head in his hands.

This was supposed to be a joyful reunion, at least, that was what I had imagined. Tabitha was supposed to be uninjured and awake; she was supposed to finally reunite with Silas. But instead, I was met with confusion and overwhelming thoughts. Freedom did nothing to calm the raging war inside my heart, the flames of which were scarier than any *Breeders*, more frightening than any bottomless pit. The anxiety and anger were uncontrollable, and the darkness that had given birth so many lunations ago had its grip not only on my tendrils of light, but on my flesh. I felt it there, tightening its grip on my heart, my fears now shifting to a physical pain. Sayah had blindly risked her life and confronted Bakunax head-on, and I could not find the courage to look her in the eye, to tell her the truth that I was a coward, and how her nature terrified me so.

I squinted into the sunlight, finding the shape of her silhouette as she rested in the perfect crevice between the nape of Obsydora's neck. Nox was beside her, his hand resting in the middle of her back, as a reassurance she did not roll in her slumber. The sapphire dragon's wings were fully extended, and as the light refracted off her scales, multiple waves of rainbows were scattered all around us, and I couldn't help but mourn the beauty I knew surrounded me. Because I wanted to feel a shred of relief that everyone else seemed to be experiencing, I wanted to be wholly present in the moment.

But the doubt had already spread its plague, consuming all other things. I doubted Sayah would forgive me for my most inner thoughts, because they did not begin after *Mãe's* death. No, it had been many lunations before…Perhaps the first time I witnessed the other elven children in the Woodland's treating her differently, as I witnessed the fear in their eyes. It was the fear of the unknown, of anything different. The worst part is that I knew better; I knew my sister better than anyone. She was not a monster, yet the fear embedded in my mind festered and grew, despite knowing she was not a being to be feared. I still found myself casting doubt on her actions.

What would Sayah think if I told her, if I revealed everything? Would she hate me?

"*Marked One*, I can feel your anxiety," Fraener grumbled, his deep tone vibrating beneath me, causing me to jump. "Go on and state your troubles. I can only imagine what that ghastly dragon must have said to you."

I blinked, absorbing his words.

"Bakunax is no longer considered a dragon, Fraener. Terragorn would gut you on the spot if he heard you call him by the name of your brethren."

He puffed a large amount of smoke, temporarily blinding me as I inhaled the fumes, triggering an unwarranted coughing fit.

"Terragorn has always been a stickler for titles; not I. It's not about their species, but a being's character. And we can all agree that Bakunax is rotten to the core," Fraener quipped, shaking his massive head as he dipped into the clouds momentarily.

"Oh, is that so?" I murmured, a grin playing on the edge of my lips. When our crew first encountered the horde, Fraener, in fact, did care about such things. He was concerned with titles and viewed most other species as inferior. *What could have changed his mind?* "You seem a bit different from when I first met you, Fraener. What did I miss?" My question nearly caught in my throat, a lump of emotion forming.

"You missed many things," The stumpy dragon barked, flapping his wings several times before gliding on the air current. "But you were also missed," Fraener snapped quietly, and his admittance returned the grin to my face.

"Who missed me?" I leaned forward on his spine, as close as I could manage without the wind snagging me in the process. "It couldn't have been you. Maybe Sayah, most definitely Enid... But not you. Oh, I know!" Turning to look behind me, the burnt orange dragon that got under Fraener's skin was behind us, like a mother goose watching over her brood. "Terragorn would've missed me, and Obsydora!"

"What utter complete nonsense!" he growled, his body shaking with anger. "Since when have you ever conversed with the old lizard?"

I threw my head back, laughing. *I knew Fraener would only hear Terragorn's name, the dragon he both despised and revered.* And I finally felt it; a bit of happiness trickled into my soul, the golden liquid leaking through the cracks of my hardened exterior. And it was followed by immense guilt. *Am I allowed to be happy when Tabitha can't even open her eyes, she can't smile or laugh? I was so overwhelmingly tired of feeling sad; I was desperate to feel happiness, even if it was just a lousy imitation of the real thing.*

"You might be a *Marked One*, but I am not afraid to scare you a bit. Fraener might catch you when you fall, maybe not. I wouldn't test that theory." My head snapped up at the female's rumble, and Obsydora was now adjacent to me. "We approach the border of the five kingdoms, child." She tipped her head forward, indicating there was something up ahead that I could not see.

"Let us begin." A thundering voice came from directly behind, sending goosebumps up and down my forearms. Terragorn had silently joined us, the hatchlings at his sides. They had grown tremendously since I last saw the adolescent beings up close, their true colors peeking through their black, iridescent scales in the sunlight. "We are changing formation. You two will need to take the lead position so the *Marked Ones* can open the barrier."

"You want us to do what exactly?!" Sayah retorted, and I shifted my body to face hers. She wore the same expression as I, wide-eyed and full of shock; the only difference was that her features were still puffy from sleep. Nox sat behind her, his focus not on the conversation at all but the giant fog that stretched across the vast waters.

"*Marked Ones* are the only beings who are permitted to cross," Fraener snapped his response before Terragorn could get another word out. "It is why Bakunax wanted you two specifically—you both carry the most power within your scrawny frames out of what is left of the *Marked Ones*. Let your power flow out of you and into the barrier. This will create a doorway, and if done successfully, we should all be able to enter."

"What vital information; maybe share with the entire group before arrival," Enid shouted, her head popping up and over Terragorn's, her hair whipping in the wind. "We have an injured being who needs help, and we flew for several days, and we are not sure this will work."

My face burned at Enid's anger, and I wanted more than anything not to disappoint her.

"We can do it." I turned to Sayah, whose mouth was agape.

"Ornella, you're in no shape to open a gate to the other side," my sister complained, her voice laced with worry. "I'll do it by myself."

"No, Sayah," I snapped, shaking my head. "Look at the massive size of Terragorn; there's no possible way you can create a hole wide enough to fit through on your own." I raised a brow as she studied the mystical fog, her eyes already defeated. She knew I was right.

"There's no time to waste." Sayah patted Obsydora, who was gliding over the seawater, her iridescent wings fully expanded. We all approached the mist, which, to my surprise, was not actually a mist at all. It resembled the inside of the *Videira*, the elves' sacred vine. Multiple glowing orbs moved about the river above the sea, leaving a trail of haze in their wake. This was why, from a distance, the spell resembled clouds. The *Ligação Mágica* nipped at the threshold of the mist, the green and gold swirls seemingly reluctant to not have the ability to cross.

I put out my hands, my palms sweaty.

Why was I nervous? It was second nature to me to use my power for the betterment of those around me. This time was no different. And yet

I beheld Sayah, and there was a newfound confidence in her stance, and a fierce look etched into her brow.

My hands shook, and I started to break out into a cold sweat.

Relax, I can do this. I just needed to pretend I was back in Alizeh, and I had gifted energy to someone who was injured and recovering at one of the clinics.

With my eyes closed, I let the gentle flow of energy flow out of my core, and into the barrier between us and another world entirely.

The orbs were dipped in multicolored hues, though their flesh was translucent. As my power flowed into the mist alongside Sayah's, they spun in a circular motion, shaking with intensity until my eyes went wide with discovery; I could see through the barrier and onto the other side.

I nearly fell off of Fraener at the shock of what lay beyond the five kingdoms.

For it was not what, but *who.*

A celestial being stared back at me, with eyes that were carved from the stars.

Chapter Twenty-Nine

Sayah

The veil between the two spaces came undone, and the hole inside the mist grew at an alarming rate until it was large enough to fit even Terragorn through nature's doorway. Symbols of light flew by me, sparking in the air. It was in complete contrast to the black that seeped from my fingertips. The green and gold swirls of magic swirled around Obsydora and me, creating an ethereal display of color and magic.

I could feel the stares of my friends around me, creating a target of unwanted expectations on my back. I knew it wasn't intentional, but it added to the weight of the pressure nonetheless. Tabitha needed us, and we were taking a considerable risk by venturing into the unknown in search of answers. The reason why I trusted this was the answer to healing her was that the dragons were so sure of it; they said those who resided on the other side of this enchanted barrier could heal and save her.

Waves lapped at the sapphire dragon's sides, salt water spraying up and into my field of vision. My power was testing its limits, the pressure building in my palms as it released out and into the open. It seeped into the wall of magic, mixing with Ornella's white light. I glanced at my sister, and a lump formed in my throat. I knew I needed to put everything I had into opening the barrier. She was skin and bone, her complexion cracked and peeling from the immediate overexposure to the sun. I hardly recognized her.

My heart ached for the young woman she used to be, the quiet confidence she exuded from the instant she was in your company. Before we left Alizeh for the first time, her entire presence was filled with color and life. But her time inside Mount Auberon had drained her of that vibrancy, and she was now a shell of the person I had once known.

It felt as if I was standing next to a stranger.

And on the other side of the threshold, I felt unfamiliar eyes glued to my figure. But my grip on my control was slipping, and I needed to focus on what was important—getting Tabitha across to the other side, the unknown.

"Go on, I can't hold it for too long." I winced, the muscles in my forearms already spent.

I heard a buzz in my ear, followed by a grumbling. "What if they try to attack us the minute we are inside?" Kazumi's raspy voice felt oddly comforting in the intense moment.

"Sprinkle some fairy dust on them, and have Brom light it on fire," I said through gritted teeth. "Seriously, please *move*."

Kazumi sighed, and the sound of her wings fluttering beside me dissipated along with her reply. "You heard her—start flapping your wings and cross."

The feisty fairy did have a point. What if they attacked? And I couldn't quite let go of the comment mentioned by Bakunax; dragons hate Marked Ones. What was he referring to?

Terragorn moved first, wading through the ocean. As he entered through the barrier, his body was pushed back, as if he were fighting against an invisible force; a weight was pressing down on his massive frame. But after several tries, he swam directly through to the other side, followed by the rest of the horde. All that was left were Nox, Ornella, and me, as we stood on top of Obsydora and Fraener.

"You go through first, and hold your ground as you switch to the other side. That way, Obsydora can cross the threshold as well," I directed with urgency. There was an awkward pause, a buildup of tension. It felt as though our usual dynamic was reversed, and that feeling was unsettling. My twin struggled to keep her arms raised; her lips were parted in exasperation. My focus flickered back and forth between her and the unknown, as I was torn on how to force her to take action. *Bless the vine, the opening was growing smaller by the instant.*

"Sayah, you go first. I can hold it," she said with a failing confidence. I saw it there in her emerald eyes as she fought against her fatigue; my sister was in denial. She did not understand the gravity of her situation, how famished she was—how it was mostly my power holding the entrance open, and even at that, my own strength was waning. And my heart was breaking for her, for her already broken soul. *Mãe* would have collapsed from the mere sight of what my twin had become, from the obvious torture she'd endured. It was the immense amount of guilt that kept me level-headed; I needed to do what was right by my sister; for once in my life, I needed not to hesitate and make the right decision.

"Fraener, go." I glared at the jade dragon, who said nothing, because he wasn't a fool. He knew.

After several seconds, he moved of his own accord, much to the disdain of Ornella.

"I said I can do it!" she cried, and her weary face held the look of betrayal.

Fraener struggled against the misty spell; his short, robust figure splashed in the water, the orbs surrounding him pushing his figure back into our territory. Ornella cried out, and a blast of white light shot from her hands, and Fraener leapt at the opportunity and crossed over inside her gift of energy.

I watched my sister's back as she crossed, determined to see her safe and sound. But as soon as my focus shifted from my task to my sister, my arms began to give out from the strenuous flow of power seeping from my core. "Obsydora, it's now or never." I strained as I yelled the words, and the circle of mist began to dissipate, along with the view of my friends on the other side.

She dove into the mist, and I screamed in pain as I tried to force the wall of moving orbs to let me pass. The barrier's spell was excruciatingly painful; the spheres of color held an electrical current that bled into your senses when touched.

We somehow managed to tumble through the ancient spell and onto the other side, and into the unknown lands.

My mouth was agape as I took in the ocean and unfamiliar faces before me, because it was missing a vital part of how our world exists—the *Ligação Mágica.*

"Where's the land's magic?" I questioned, mystified.

"You won't find magic here," a hollow voice echoed between the spaces, and I finally found the courage to face the beings head-on.

We were still in ocean water, but not too far off in the distance, there was land. A mystical castle that was so tall the tips of its towers seemed to touch the clouds, as rolling hills surrounded it. I ripped my eyes away from the scenery and to the unknown species. They awaited us on a vessel, a fleet ship to be exact. Its white flags flapped in the wind, a drastic change from the looming black sails of the *Thereon's* ships.

Each being removed their hood, revealing their features. An audible gasp was heard uttered from several lips at the sight of the strangers. Their ears were pointed, sharp, and elongated. All of their eyes were a pure black; it was as if you were staring into the galaxy, and it peered back in wonder. The ethereal beings had varying shades to their complexion, from onyx to a snowy white. But the species all shared the golden, flaked freckles across their cheeks and noses, as if the stars themselves were embedded in their skin.

My eyes skimmed them for similarities; Ornella and I had a similar build, though we were not quite as tall and not nearly as regal. These beings held the truth of our ancestry in the grasp of their fingertips, which I possessed a burning desire to discover.

This was our birth mother's origins; mine and my sister's identity lay hidden, buried beneath their soil, their oceans.

"Greetings." A being stepped forward, the same woman with the eerie voice who spoke moments before. Her lavender hair cascaded out from beneath her hood as she bowed to us accordingly. "We are the *Estrella,* the first species shaped by the *Creator,* and the origin of all beings with power. The five kingdoms know our kind as the *Marked Ones.*"

"How did you know we would be here?" Nox spoke from behind me, and I jumped. I had forgotten entirely of his presence, a blush heating my cheeks and the tips of my ears.

The woman nodded, as if she expected this response. "I have the gift of sight." She walked with an air about her, her head held high. She was the epitome of grace. "Your friend is in dire need of attention; all questions will be answered in due time." Her demeanor shifted abruptly after she answered, and she was now looking up at the clouds. My mind might have been playing tricks on me, but out of the corner of my eye, I thought I witnessed her lip quiver. "We must quicken our haste back to the castle; we can discuss more after you've all had a proper meal." She then slightly bowed and gestured to the other beings who accompanied her. "I am Lady Gwyneth, and this is Tagen and Demetri. Those whom you see on this ship are the beings I trust. Remember their faces."

Tagen removed his hood, and his head full of flames would make him easy to identify. My gaze shifted to Demetri, whose face looked as though it had never held an expression; his pale skin was morbid, and the dark circles under his eyes were troublesome.

The others moved about, readying the ship and hoisting the sails.

"It is advised that the horde does not fly through our skies, for security measures," Demetri said, his voice underwhelmingly monotone. "Lady

Gwyneth would prefer you travel with us from this point on, as the dragons may bring too much attention to your presence."

My ears perked up to what he was implying.

"Do you mean to say, not everyone knows of us opening the barrier?" I asked with caution, and suddenly *Mãe's* letter popped into my head. *These were the same beings who murdered my paternal parents. Of course, there would be enemies; I am upset with myself for allowing myself to feel indifferent toward them—I should be angry.*

"That's precisely what he is implying, so we need to get a move on." The man named Tagen offered me his hand to help me onto the vessel that was now a few feet away from where Obsydora treaded in the sea. "I'll be escorting your lovely friends to a secret location; it's best if the horde isn't known of just yet."

Obsydora clicked her throat, and Terragorn shook his head in her direction; it felt extremely accusatory. "We will obey the orders of those who know these lands; now get off my back, so that I may properly stretch my spine."

Silas was first off the old grump, with Tabitha cradled in his arms. "Help her, *please*." He was looking directly at Lady Gwyneth when he said this, the desperation tangible in his tone.

"There is a way, but she will not be entirely the same. She will not be the woman you once knew, but reborn. Are you okay with this?" She studied Silas, waiting to see how he would respond.

"If it means she lives, she could lose her memory, and I would still be satisfied knowing that her heart still beats in her chest. I look forward to the new memories we shall create together." My heart leapt at Silas's answer, and I looked at him in a new light. He was willing to give up her memories of him if that's what it took to save her.

"Do not worry, she will still have her memories of you." A soft smile played on Lady Gwyneth's lips, her gaze momentarily shifting between Silas and Tabitha. "But she may act differently; you'll understand soon enough. We will need to start her awakening."

Chapter Thirty
Sayah

"Awakening?" I asked as I leaned over the starboard side of the railing, the vessel slowly starting to take on speed. Tabitha was escorted to the cabin of the ship beneath the deck, where several beings were tending to her the best they could.

Lady Gwyneth stood beside me, worry lines creasing her face as she scanned the beach ahead. "Your friend there, she is one of us—she is an *Estrella*. She comes from our realm, *Paraiso.*"

I shifted my weight from one leg to the other. "Her name is Tabitha, and how is that possible? How could she cross the border?"

"I have formed my own conclusions," she said under her breath, eyes narrowed. "At the time of her disappearance, she would have been too young to use her powers to open the gate. This means that more than likely, someone opened the gateway for her and let her out."

"You have the gift of sight; can you not see the culprit?"

A laugh bubbled up from out of her chest, surprising us both. "That is not the way my gift of sight works, darling. I see important events; these cannot be changed. At least, this is from my own experience." She dusted off the hem of her shirt and turned away from the sea to meet my gaze. "But the small, mundane moments. You can change those. And I would like to believe that if someone were to make enough little changes, the imminent events could be prevented or swayed as well."

I mulled over this, biting the inside of my cheek. The wind nipped my face; little splashes of salt water tickled my cheeks and hair. I leaned over the siding and peered out into the ocean, half expecting to see the ripples of the *Ligação Mágica* dancing beneath its surface.

"And what of our land's magic? Why is it not here?" I peeked at her from beneath my eyelashes, curious to see if she would tell me the whole truth, or just bits and pieces.

"Hmmm, that is a complicated answer." Lady Gwyneth twisted away from me, now looking in the direction of my friends who were up on the forecastle. I glanced over at Ornella, who seemed to have brightened a bit now that Enid was by her side. And the fact that the ogress baked her cookies, and my sister ate one now, her features relaxed. She was not entirely herself, but this was the first moment I had witnessed her show any happiness. I suppose that was the power of what a dessert could do.

My stomach grumbled in jealousy.

"Define magic for me," she commanded, and I raised my brows, clearly caught off guard. *Answering a question with a question because she most likely did not want to answer. Lady Gwyneth was indeed cunning.* Her fingers brushed the edge of the ship as we approached the shoreline. "Nothing in this world is free. The more one connects with the magic, the more one becomes gradually complacent to the threat lying beneath. Would you agree with this?" she continued. "And I cannot think of anything more terrifying than a soul willing to trade its independence for a false sense of security. Yet here we stand, witnessing the evolution of all species giving in to the ease of comfort as they snap their fingertips, reciting spell after spell, unwilling to learn basic skills. What would happen if the land's magic in your world were to disappear? What then?"

I scratched my chin, dumbfounded. "Now I'm more confused than I was before I asked. Was that your goal?"

Lady Gwyneth laughed, shaking her head in amusement. "The truth is no one knows for sure why things have played out the way they have. But my personal theory, which will get me into trouble, is that magic is just a tool for the *Creator* to control lesser beings with." Her words shockingly stung, and I looked down at the soaked wooden floorboards. "And for the *Estrella*," she paused, waiting for my gaze to shift back to hers to continue. "The *Creator* does not need the land's magic to control us. They do so by using our gifts against us."

I raised my brows, rubbing my face as I processed. "That does indeed sound like that point of view would get you into trouble—at the very least, perhaps make a few enemies. I'm beginning to see why the others were not alerted to our arrival."

She nodded in agreement and sighed. "They will be aware soon enough. Your friend's awakening will inform all of *Paraiso* that you have made an appearance. So, before then, we will prepare Tabitha for the change, and let all those who have traveled take a warm bath and nourish their bodies. Because the instant certain beings know of your presence, that is when the dice of fate are at play. And I'm not ready to roll my hand just yet."

The vessel quite suddenly began to rock back and forth, as the sound of the anchor dropping into the ocean was heard splashing into the water from the bow of the ship.

We had arrived.

Chapter Thirty-One

Sayah

We were seated at a massive table, nearly the same length as Ter-ragorn's tale. Everything inside the castle was adorned in either silver or gold, overly accentuating the *Estrellas'* prestigious lineage. It was a far cry from the table inside of Ulfred's quaint home that sat beside the lighthouse in Erebus. That table wasn't even a table at all; it was a grand piano, with a dusty cloth thrown over the top for good measure. Sitting here inside this grand room that I knew nothing about, other than the fact that my birth mother, Etienne, once lived in these castle walls, I felt out of place.

Brom was scarfing down several chicken legs, bones and all, in front of me with no remorse for his lack of table etiquette. This alone pulled at the corners of my mouth as I fought the urge to smile.

"You need to eat," Nox whispered from my side, resting a hand on my knee beneath the table.

"I know." I instinctively grabbed a bread roll from the mountain of food placed with precision in bowls and dishes that were also lavished in gold and intricate patterns. A memory of *Mãe* sitting in front of me at the ceremony's banquet flashed before my eyes; her judgmental stare as I was willing to stuff the entire container of bread rolls into my leather bag to take back to the cottage for snacking later. I missed her with every fiber of my being. But I needed to hold it together and not let this wave of grief take hold of my heart. *Remember what she told you: you need to eat when given the opportunity, because another meal was never guaranteed. And especially not now, not when you're on the run, not when a war is on the brink.*

I chewed slowly, replaying the words in my head of Lady Gwyneth over and over.

The Estrella are shaped by the Creator's hands, not born. We are the first species ever to exist, and our lifespans are that of hundreds of lifetimes for an elf. When an Estrella is reincarnated, their power is influenced by what that individual needed most in their previous life.

Hmmm, interesting.

Ornella and I were blessed with the gift of energy manipulation that split in two during our time in our mother's womb. I tapped my fork on the wooden table, perplexed. *What precisely happened to my sister and me in a previous life that would give us such a gift?*

"You going to eat that?" Brom pointed at my plate with some sort of unidentified meat in his hand, the juices dripping onto the table.

"She is, so hands off." Nox was quick on the reply, and he glared at me with an eyebrow raised.

"*Bless the vine*, Nox. I'm eating. See?" I took an exaggerated bite of my chicken leg, stuffing as much as I could into one bite.

The one Lady Gwyneth called Demetri sat on the other side of Nox and began to fill his plate without filling the silence with pleasantries.

"What's your gift?" Kazumi popped out from behind a large dish, and she was the last being I would have assumed would be the one doing the small talk; that was usually Silas. I scanned the table for his familiar head of sandy hair, but it dawned on me that he and Caelan skipped supper to be by Tabitha's side in the infirmary. *I'll have to save some food for them to bring later.* Before I could forget, I filled a napkin full of several items and wrapped it carefully before resting it in my lap.

"I make Lady Gwyneth's problems disappear," he grinned, and the smile didn't reach the corners of his mouth. His eyes were like galaxies with dimmed stars, not bright like the others I've seen. "And my own problems," he added, as if this were an afterthought, as he bit into a chicken breast.

"And your friends?" Enid questioned, her eyes narrowed on Tagen, who was seated several chairs down, conversing with those who seemed to be his peers. The ogress was beside Ornella, who was on my right. She had remained quiet, distant. My eyes flickered to her hand, which was tightly gripping the arm of her chair.

"Oh, Tagen's? Thought manipulation." Demetri shrugged, taking another bite.

My eyes went wide. *Thought manipulation?* That was the last gift of power that I would have guessed. From his build, I figured it was strength-related. The man with fiery hair could manipulate thoughts, and Demetri could make someone disappear. Why was Lady Gwyneth keeping this sort of company by her side? I tried to stab several peas on my plate with my fork, but I was unsuccessful. *What must they have endured in their previous lives to be blessed with such gifts?*

"When you two are finished, I would very much like to show you around the castle," Lady Gwyneth said from behind my chair, and even Nox slightly jumped next to me.

"Your stealth is something else; my father would like you," Nox grumbled, and I jabbed an elbow in his ribcage to keep him quiet.

"Absolutely, we would be more than happy to oblige!" I shoved the food in my lap into Nox's and mouthed, *"For Silas and Caelan,"* as I pushed out my chair to leave the table. Ornella still said nothing, but followed suit.

We strolled through the corridors, taking in the full splendor of the enchanting scenery that was the ancient castle. Trees grew from the ceiling—each adorned with twinkling lights that captured the merriment of the evening. The remaining sunlight cast a warm glow about the chamber, softening the tension that had lingered from the previous engagement. Ornella and I inspected the paintings along the hallways, the figures of nobility all seated in the throne room. Lady Gwyneth let us dawdle, a soft smile playing at the edge of her lips as her hands were casually behind her back.

After turning several corners, I halted in front of a large mural surrounding the garden's entrance. It was a gruesome battle scene, not fitting for the gorgeous foliage just outside the doorway. In the illustration, there were kings from each nobility with both hands extended into the sky, desperately reaching toward a glowing orb. Their clothes were stained with their comrades' blood, the king's expressions in awe of the luminescent light, ignorant of the death and decay encompassing them.

"What are they reaching for?" I asked, bewildered by the look of lust and desire sculpted beautifully into the monarch's features.

Ornella squinted; her brows furrowed. She was also perplexed by the painting. "Oh!" Her head turned to the priestess, understanding wading inside her emerald eyes. "The kings are reaching for the *Creator.*"

She stepped forward, and the amusement in her face vanished.

"I'm afraid not. They are reaching toward an abomination of a weapon, forged by the original *Estrella*—or as you would say, *Marked Ones.*" Her voice echoed through the various passageways on either side of us, the ominous tone reverberating deep within the fortress. She moved as if in a trance, her demeanor evolving to an emotion I had not yet recognized. Lady Gwyneth's awareness of our presence seemed to dissipate; her pupils dilated as a sharp inhale filled her lungs. Her hand mimicked that of the kings in the painting, fingers grazing the painted orb above our heads. "That is the *Saudade* to the *Marked Ones*; the monarchs commonly know it as the *soul shield.*" Her lip quivered, a deep yearning swirling inside her dark irises.

"*The soul shield*?" Ornella and I whispered in unison, sparking the movement of Lady Gwyneth. Her captivation with the illustration abruptly ended, and she snatched her hand away from the mural in disgust.

There were many things Lady Gwyneth chose to hide from us; she made it seem as if it were for our own safety. She kept our entire crew to one side of the castle, telling us not to venture too far without her permission or without her convenient escorts. But the look in her eyes just now sent a shiver of goosebumps down my spine. *What other secrets lie hidden within these walls? Or perhaps I should say, within the barriers in her mind?* It was impossible to connect with her *Gavinhas* using the *Ligação Mágica* to see what she was plotting because they did not exist in these lands.

"Come," she beckoned, opening the glass doors to the garden and entering the foliage without so much as a glance back in our direction. Her willowy figure was easy to spot over the green shrubbery, her lilac waves flowing in the wind behind her as she moved with purpose. We quickened our pace, afraid that we would lose her in the maze of vegetation. Yellow daffodils bobbed their heads as we passed by, reminding me of *Mãe's* cottage back in Alizeh. Another twinge of pain pulled at my heart as it often did every instant I recalled *Mãe* and our simple life in the Woodlands—before the *Thereon* had attacked the night of our ceremony.

There were many paintings in the garden, and one struck me with confusion as I recognized the boy sitting beneath a mother and father-like figure. His eyes were multicolored, with a look of disdain etched along his features. My focus shifted to the woman whose hand rested on his shoulder; she had greyish eyes and long, white waves. The stranger shared the same heart-shaped face with rounded lips as my twin and me. I instinctively reached for the portrait displayed beautifully in a bed of pink carnations; my fingers gently caressing the painting, feeling its texture as if it were her skin. It was the mother I never had the privilege of knowing; an untimely death because she chose our lives over her own. My cheeks felt cold, and I brushed them with the back of my hand, surprised to find tears there. I had been crying.

"What happened to her?" My feet were planted in the soil, as if I had taken root; my desire to know her tragic story grew and weaved its way around my heart. I could not be unearthed until I knew what had become of the woman who had protected us with such a sacrifice.

Out of the corner of my vision, I saw white waves of hair. Ornella paused, staring at the face of Etienne. When I fully turned to see her expression, I was shocked to find one of anger.

"Tell me of him, Lady Gwyneth. I need to know why our mother left our family to start a new one; why did she abandon Ein?" Her voice was full of venom, full of hate.

"Ornella, what are you saying?" I twisted back to the painting to try to fully comprehend her attack on Etienne. "We do not have another sibling."

Her head whipped in my direction so fast my heart stuttered from the waves of hostility suddenly emanating from her aura. "Oh, but we do. This was Etienne's family before she met our father, Ciaran. I must know why. Why did she leave her home and risk everything for another man? I must know why it was worth it to her."

Lady Gwyneth stood next to Ornella, her face expressionless. "Etienne and Magnus were paired together by their relations; it was not a happy union." She shifted her feet on the stone she stood on, looking to the garden's entryway. "They were not in love; it was a match to unify power. That is common for our species."

"She abandoned her son because she did not love his father?" Ornella's voice rang with disappointment. "So many horrid outcomes came from her decision."

"Etienne hated Magnus, and he hated her. She fled *Paraiso,* not with the intention of finding a lover. She left for her own peace and safety. I will admit that there was a shred of selfishness in her decision to do so. But I feel if I were to be in her position, I would have done the same." Her eyes, made of stars, narrowed at Ornella. "Do not be so quick to judge, child. She endured far more than she should have from Magnus."

"But to purposefully abandon your own child." My sister's voice broke. "I do not understand what she could have been thinking."

"She stayed as long as she did because of him," Lady Gwyneth murmured, eyes closed. "But Magnus raised Ein to hate his mother. Words were manipulated, and lies were told. Etienne could no longer take the mistreatment, so one night, she crossed the barrier and left."

"Why are you acting like this, Ornella?" I faced her head-on, forcing her to make eye contact with me. "Some things are out of our control. She did not mean for everything to happen this way."

"But because she left, *Mãe* is dead. Her son, our half-brother, is the one who murdered her. Can you not see how I would feel conflicted?"

I staggered back, bracing myself on the edge of one of the many raised flower beds. "It can't be!" I sobbed, shaking my head in disbelief. "Why, why would he do such a thing? I don't understand...if we are family, what would cause him to murder one of his own?"

"Because he doesn't view us as family!" Ornella shouted back, her face beet red. "We are nothing more than a nuisance to Ein; he believes we stole his gifts from him, his birthright. So don't you see, Sayah!?" She stepped forward, and I flinched back. "If Etienne had never left, we would not have been born. And *Mãe* would still be alive!"

I paused mid-thought, her words like a direct slap to the face.

"You think it better we never existed?" My eyes searched the garden for answers, but I found none. Only my seething sister, with her fists balled up at her sides, and Lady Gwythen, who wore the most sorrowful expression. "I'm sorry, but I can't agree with you. Because even though *Mãe* died a terrible death, I made so many wonderful memories with her. It was a privilege to exist in the same lifetime as she did, even if our time together was short. I'm sorry, Ornella."

The whites of her eyes were red, and her jaw was clenched. "You. You're just like our birth mother, Etienne." Ornella fumed, pointing her index finger at my chest. "You never make the right decisions. And I'm tired of the grief you cause me. I'm tired of the heavy burden on my chest of having to take care of myself, and you, too. It's been like this since we bloomed—since we were born." My twin licked her lips, readying her choice of weapon, the most lethal: her words. "You could have prevented *Mãe's* death, Sayah. And while I'm at it, the kingdom of Alizeh blames you for attacking their army the night of our ceremony, because you did exactly that."

I was frozen in place, unable to move, to breathe.

"I found you that night, surrounded by the military aid dispatched as reinforcements against the *Thereon* attacking the elves at the vine. Your eyes were black as night, and you had drained the entire brigade of nearly all their energy, and their *Gavinhas* flickered, as if they were about to pass."

My face contorted, a whimper escaping my lips. "I never meant for that to happen, Ornella. I'm so sorry; please believe me."

A flicker of pity escaped her features, but she quickly turned her face to the side, away from both Lady Gwyneth and me. "I know you didn't mean for it to happen. But neither did Etienne, and look at where self-serving choices get you."

My mouth opened and closed, but no words came. Because I had nothing to say that would make everything okay, to make everything right. This was her truth, and it nearly broke me. *I was a monster in her eyes; I was the cause of all her life woes.*

"Sayah, Ornella, perhaps we can continue this discussion later. It's time to prepare for Tabitha's awakening, and I'll be able to explain more about the *Estrella* and what that means."

Ornella moved first, walking down the path that led to the main corridor.

Lady Gwyneth put her hand on my shoulder, giving it a light squeeze. "Give yourself a few minutes to compose yourself. Take the time you need before following." She sauntered behind Ornella, her lavender waves swinging at her waist.

I looked down, tears blotting my vision.

"Oh, and dear," she called out to me, her voice tender. I hadn't realized that she had paused and was observing me from the doorframe. "No one can choose their fate, Sayah. You can't change fate's course because it is already known; all paths lead to the same ending."

I bit my lip, contemplating. She left me standing there alone as she followed after Ornella, and soon I was with only the paintings of those whom I knew nothing about, judging me with their unblinking eyes.

Chapter Thirty-Two

Ornella

I thought that if I were honest with Sayah, if I revealed the truths that had chained themselves to my heart, I could relieve myself of some of the pain. But now, in place of the anger and bitterness, guilt swelled inside me, filling the cracks and crevices of my armor that life's unavoidable tragedies leave behind.

We were in a room with large glass-stained windows, while Tabitha lay in the bed, tossing and turning in a fitful sleep. Attendants put cold clothes on her head as she broke out in a heavy sweat. The look of fear etched into her features as her prison fell from the top of the cavern, disappearing in the fog, was a recurring nightmare for me. It had taken the place of seeing *Mãe's* lifeless body beneath closed eyes, as I had found her there that night before finding Sayah. I thought it had been a dream at first, but after time had passed, I realized that the trauma was so profound for me that my brain had blocked it out for quite some time.

I pinched my hand, willing myself not to give in to my memories. *Tabitha was still here; she was living and breathing. What happened to Mãe would not occur to her.*

Lady Gwyneth walked in, along with several new faces I did not recognize. Their presence immediately shifted the mood of the room; their tendrils of light were immense, heavy. I was still getting used to their soul-reflecting eyes; the lights that shimmered inside them were beautiful yet terrifying.

They approached Tabitha, each laying a hand on her.

"Ornella, come." Lady Gwyneth requested my presence, the authority trickling through. I approached her side, where she was now kneeling beside my friend, who was in obvious pain. "When awakened, an *Estrella* can use their powers more effectively; they have better control and can heal at a faster rate. This is why we must speed up this process for Tabitha." She then met my gaze, a wistful expression on the corners of her mouth. "But she will not look the same as before; she will have our mark, our eyes. It is how we can tell if one has awakened or not."

I looked at Tabitha carefully, a twinge of sadness tugging on my chest. "She has beautiful blue eyes. I would hate to see them change."

"I understand that feeling; I had a difficult time coming to terms with my awakening as well. I avoided mirrors for many lunations," she whispered, and I heard the longing in her tone. "There are a few rare *Estrellas* who can control their change and switch between the two. Etienne was one of the lucky few who kept her original eye color."

My focus shifted to Sayah, who lingered in the shadows of the room, near the threshold. "Interesting." This was all I could manage to say, as my eyes focused on a piece of lint on my linen gown.

"Lady Gwyneth, let's begin," a man across from me stated. Silas moved closer, with Caelan standing with him for what I assumed to be emotional support. She had her hand on his shoulder, with furrowed brows. My gaze momentarily shifted to where Nox stood behind them, his arms crossed. He was doing everything he could to hold himself together as he watched his beloved sister writhing in pain.

The group of *Estrella* closed their eyes, and mine went wide as their *Gavinhas* began to shift, the waves of light from each individual pulled to Tabitha's center, blending into her soul and wrapping around her core. For an instant, the world around us went utterly still, quiet. And then the sound all came back at once, flooding and overwhelming my senses as a bright light pulsed around Tabitha, blinding my field of vision for several seconds.

"What happened?"

"We synchronized our souls with Tabitha's," Lady Gwyneth said, looking over my friend's body intently. Her body had stopped tossing and turning, and she was no longer holding the expression of pain in her features. "Her *Gavinhas* will heal first, following her bruises and broken bones."

I stared at Lady Gwyneth, the question on the tip of my tongue, but I was unable to ask.

"No, we are not immortal, Ornella. The only immortal I know is the *Creator*." She abruptly stood, holding her hand out for me to take. I obliged, and she helped me to my feet. "Let's let Tabitha rest, and we can visit when she awakes. We had to wait to start the ceremony until her *Gavinhas* were strong enough to handle the change; if too weak, an awakening can be detrimental."

The more she spoke, the more questions I had than answers. And the question screaming in my head was still yet to be answered.

"She'll be okay, though?" I asked the most crucial question at the moment.

Lady Gwyneth raised a brow and then smiled. "Yes, Ornella. She will be okay. I have seen it."

Chapter Thirty-Three

Tabitha

I had forgotten how it felt to be alive; to feel the blush rising to my cheeks, the warmth of someone else's touch, the sounds of nature surrounding me, the feeling of overwhelming peace blooming throughout my chest. As my vision came into focus, the pulse of my heartbeat quickened at the sight of him. There he was, and as he stood before me, it was as if he had been cast out of the pure ecstasy from my dreams; his tendrils of light creating a halo of illumination around his figure.

I did not care where I was or who the strangers gathered around me; all I saw was him. The man who my soul called out to day and night, the man who I craved more than my own freedom from the hell I had been cast in; he was the one my flesh craved, the one I was bound to for eternity. A single brush of his fingertips on my lips would send me into a bliss unknown by most.

"Silas," I whispered, the word lingering on the edge of my lips. The yearning in my cry was a tangible thing; I pledged my love for him out loud by simply speaking his name.

And from the sound of my plea, he was at my side in an instant, caressing my face between his callused hands. "I missed you," he murmured, wholly consumed in the moment as I gazed into the depths of his soul.

"And I, you." A river of tears cascaded down my cheeks, brought on by the overwhelming happiness that flooded my heart.

Everything that I had experienced, the pain that I had endured, the suffering. It had all been worth it, because I was now in the arms of the man who consumed all of my thoughts, the one who calmed the constant storm that waged a war inside my chest. Silas always knew what to say; his presence alone was a beacon of hope for my weary soul.

He was my mate, and I his.

And then his soft, supple lips were on mine, with an intensity that rivaled the strongest of desires known to man. His hands were entangled in my hair, and I reached for his face so that I could examine every inch of his features and brush the scar above his brow. I missed the parts of Silas that made him who he was, each and every imperfection a work of art.

"You look...different." He had markings. *Markings.* Silas had finally fought and won his first fight, and by the number of swirls on his arms, it was a formidable opponent.

A wide smile spread across his face, and his golden eyes sparkled. "You look a little different, too."

"I do?" My hands fluttered to my face, worried. "What's different?"

A woman with lavender hair and eyes like I had never seen before came to my side and placed a jeweled mirror in my hands. "To heal your wounds, we had to awaken your powers fully. When this change takes place, your eyes change." As I went to lift the mirror to examine my face, she stopped me. "Before you look, I need you to know that you are still you. Your outside appearance does not change who you are inside." The beautiful stranger then released her grip on my wrist, and I stared at my reflection.

It was me, and it wasn't.

I had the same cheekbones and full lips. My strawberry blonde curls needed to be tended to, and the bags under my eyes were permanent. But I did not recognize my eyes themselves; they were an onyx with blue twinkly lights inside; the golden flecks on my cheeks and nose were more pro-nounced, reflecting the sunlight reaching my ebony skin from the window.

I was beautiful; ethereal, even. But I did not feel like me, not wholly.

"I appreciate the warning. I don't think I would've handled that as gracefully if you hadn't said something beforehand." I slightly bowed my head at the woman, who nodded.

Silas squeezed my hand, giving me a gentle reassurance. "You look lovely, Tabitha."

I blushed, my focus darting down the bedsheets. "Thank you."

"Let's give Tabitha some time to rest. I'm Lady Gwyneth, by the way. And when you're ready, I know of some beings who would very much like to meet you."

I gulped, looking to Silas. He shrugged his shoulders, meaning he was just as clueless as I was. "Alright, I'll let you know when I'm ready. Everyone but Silas can leave." I grinned a toothy grin and patted the bedding next to me. "You're staying."

He barked a laugh and pushed back his sandy hair. It had grown past his eyes and was nearly to his shoulders now. A twinge of sadness burdened me, as I knew there was a lot more that I had missed in the many lunations I was held hostage.

"I wasn't going to leave, even if you asked me to." Silas winked and snuggled in close underneath the sheets. He held me there, long after everyone who was in the room had shuffled out into the hallway. I had no idea where I was or what was happening, and it was the first time in my life that I genuinely did not care. I was in the arms of the man I loved, and that was enough.

The sound of muffled voices woke me from my slumber; my head rested on Silas' chest, and the gentle thrumming of his heartbeat sent another wave of calm throughout my limbs. Two figures were in the doorway, and I had to strain my hearing to pick up on their inconspicuous exchange.

"Why do you think that is?" I recognized Ornella immediately, as worry was laced into her higher-pitched tone permanently. "How could she have fully awakened her powers without the help of the *Estrella*? None were present on the day of our ceremony."

"It is peculiar... is it not?" A woman's voice resonated in my ears; you could practically hear the wisdom that came with long life. "Perhaps there was one of our kind at the ceremony that night after all. Even if we did not see them, it is the only logical explanation. Or…" She paused, and quiet filled my dimly lit room; now all that could be heard was Silas' gentle snores.

"Lady Gwyneth," Ornella strained, and she was clearly perturbed about something unseen. "If there's something you're not telling me, now's the time to speak up. This is regarding Sayah, and she is my responsibility."

There were several beats of silence; I found myself trying to minimize my breaths. I kept my eyes closed, careful not to clench them shut to appear asleep. Time moved slowly as I awaited the conclusion of the secrets being disclosed just a few feet away.

"I have already revealed too much; you mustn't utter a word of this to anyone, *especially* your sister. Do you understand, child?" Lady Gwyneth snapped, her demeanor drastically changing within seconds. "The walls are always listening, my dear. Always." She whispered, and a lump formed in my throat as we were met with an ominous silence. *What could she mean?*

I bit my lip, fighting the urge to open my eyes. But I held it together until the sounds of their footsteps padding on the stone floor were all that could be heard, and I was left in silence.

What do I do with this information? Do I tell Sayah? Or even Silas? I contemplated my options. *Even if I say something, I don't have the whole truth; I don't have all the information.*

I stared at the entryway, wondering what other secrets had been whispered under its frame; what truths had seeped into its wooden boards. My eyes suddenly felt heavy, and I blinked several times.

I knew what must be done: the whole truth must be revealed before I can make a decision on who to tell, or if I should tell anyone at all.

My focus fluttered around the nearly barren room, and I remembered what Lady Gwyneth had mentioned to Ornella moments before; the walls were always listening. *What did she mean by that?* The large glass-stained windows seemed to stare at me; paintings of faces I did not know. But this is when I noticed their eyes; they were not of the *Estrella*. They were ordinary men, with no notable gifts or lineage to be made apparent. And this is when it occurred to me that most of their history painted on these walls, and in this castle full of secrets, was not of their own kind.

Revealing the truths of this unknown land would indeed be a challenge.

This was my last coherent thought as I pulled up the bedsheets to my chin and drifted out of consciousness, as I let sleep consume me.

Chapter Thirty-Four

Nox

My instincts told me something was off about this castle, the *Estrella*. The paintings of the past haunted my dreams, along with their eyes that held so many emotions at once; I couldn't help but think they saw through my tough-guy façade. And then, there was the entirely different issue of not knowing what powers each individual possessed. *What if they tried to hurt Sayah or one of my crew members?*

I pondered this as I leaned against one of the archways in front of the garden, waiting for the burly ogre to turn the corner. I was not going to let Lady Gwyneth and her hounds have the upper hand; I planned to flip over a few stones in my spare time. I smiled to myself, thinking of Kazumi breaking and entering all of the chambers without a single soul knowing she was ever there. Her part in our scheming was crucial, and I just loved that little feisty fairy and her loyalty to the cause—to me.

As I waited, I studied the mural encompassing the garden's entrance. The battle scene contained kings with their hands reaching toward a glowing orb, their eyes transfixed on the object as everyone surrounding them died gruesome deaths.

An image of my father's power-hungry face flashed across my mind.

His delusional beliefs sat with me these days, as we prepared for the inevitable war with the army of *Thereon* that lady Gwyneth predicted would happen in the imminent future. He called the treasure he coveted *the soul shield*, a legendary item that could grant any wish, any desire. I doubted its existence. *And even if the folklore of my childhood were to be real, what would something that powerful cost? What was the price for magic that reversed evil?* And as I looked into the depths of the eyes of the *Estrella*, I wondered. *Did they already pay that price?*

This unsettling feeling persisted as I waited for Brom to meet me at the end of the corridor; the entire castle was haunting. It was as if I were stepping into a painting of the past, waking up in the middle of a nightmare, only to realize that I had entered my dreams, and survival was my singular focus.

The ogre finally rounded the corner, and my eyes shifted to the item in his hands: an axe.

"Not your usual weapon of choice." I pointed with my chin, arms crossed.

He glanced down at the object, awkward in his grasp. "The man named Tagen handed it to me, told me to learn how to use it properly." Brom raised a brow at this, grinning. "As if I didn't know how to use an axe. I grew up in the mountains in Alun, where the giants also reside. There are many weapons and tools that I know how to use; I prefer to use my hands."

A hearty laugh unexpectedly escaped me at this, rattling my chest. I crossed my arms, scanning the long and haunting hallways. The plants that grew here in this land also made their way into the castle, the overgrown foliage spreading like a welcomed plague amongst the cemented pillars and stone.

"Do you think they are with us?" I said under my breath as we ambled our way to the pavilion. The *Estrella* were there, reviewing their battle plans for the inevitable war. We had turned down several corners and walked down several flights of stairs before Brom answered.

"I honestly do not know." The ogre scratched his chin, the hesitation evident in his features. "They are hard to read. But we should be on alert while in their presence."

Out of the corner of my eye, a vine on the castle wall moved, twisting and constricting its way through the indoor foliage. *As if it were watching, listening, waiting.*

Which of the Estrella controlled vegetation in such a way?

I patted Brom on the back hard, my reply a little too loud. "They healed Tabitha, and that is enough for me." *For now.* But the feeling of unease scratched the back of my mind, and my friend shrugged his shoulders and opened the doors to the outside.

"Lady Gwyneth seems friendly enough, and she trusts Sayah and Ornella." He gestured to the large group of warriors in front of us, preparing for war. "We have other things to worry about at the moment, and even if we have different motivations, we want the same result. To see Bakunax and his legion of *Thereon* fall." Brom's tone turned to stone, cutting through his usual chipper demeanor.

"Yes, the *Estrella* and their powers are necessary to win. Let's play nice then, shall we?" I winked at him, and he curtly nodded as we strolled over to join in on the preparations.

The inconspicuous vine slunk its way back inside the castle, past the garden, the ballroom, and the galley. It slunk all the way back to its owner, where they lay waiting.

Chapter Thirty-Five

Sayah

In the moons following my altercation with Ornella, I found myself often wandering the indoor garden, as if my soul was pulled in its direction. It reminded me of Alizeh, with the humid air and flowers dancing alongside mushrooms as you strolled by.

A bench sat in the center of its design, and sometimes I would rest on its wooden boards and pretend that *Mãe* was next to me, telling me stories of her outlandish trips from her youth, along with how the day's trivial tasks at her music academy had gone. The silence was jarring in some instances, when I would ask a question and turn only to find an empty seat, a shadow of where she should have been.

I would stare at the space, as if I could somehow conjure her spirit out of thin air. *What would she think of us and how drastically we have changed in such a short period of time? Would she be proud?*

Ornella was finally free from the *Breeders of Thereon*, and yet I couldn't have felt more distant from my twin. It was painfully evident that she avoided my company altogether; she would rather be with Enid helping plan out the food reserves—the thought of war at all created knots in my stomach. I hadn't spoken much to her since we fought in the garden in front of Lady Gwyneth that day. I wasn't sure what to say or how to remedy the situation. I longed for a scenario that would bridge the gap between us; that would bring us together again.

I ambled the narrow paths of the shrubbery, where the weathered stepping stones formed a maze of various loops and crossroads. It wasn't the vegetation that caught my attention; however, it was the art that adorned the room and nearby hallways. The paintings of memories past would send goosebumps down my spine every time I walked beneath the archway and into the vibrant forestry.

Lady Gwyneth's words struck a chord with me, replaying in my mind as I plucked a lotus flower from the ground, gently rubbing its petals between my fingers.

No one can choose their fate, Sayah. You can't change fate's course because it is already known; all paths lead to the same ending.

She spoke to me later that day, trying to give words of wisdom, I assumed. But something rattled deep within my heart disagreed, and I thought of Obsydora and how she believed in me with such certainty. She encouraged me to make the right choices, even when everyone else viewed me as a monster. *Lady Gwyneth reiterated that our gifts are chosen based on what we needed most in a previous life. What was she trying to tell me?* I studied the shade of vibrant pink on the petals and began to pluck them one by one, letting them drift to the soil at my feet.

Staring at the petals on the ground, my vision began to sharpen; my tendrils of light glowed bright and crackled like electricity around my figure. Time seemed to stand still, and my thoughts drastically shifted to someone else's; someone familiar yet new entirely.

In my vision, I was standing at the *Videira*, holding a glowing orb with colors floating in and out of its center, and I realized that what I possessed was life itself, multiple portions of entities intricately woven together to create something beautiful.

This entity was enchanting yet defied the very laws of nature; its existence questioned all that we held to be true. It was *The Soul Shield,* or known by the Estrela as the *Saudade.*

My body involuntarily moved forward, possessed by a driving force, a conviction so strong and unwavering that I knew what must be done, even if it held a significant cost. Tears formed in the corners of my eyes as I pushed the *Saudade* into the sacred vine, letting the sentient being absorb all the fragments of the chosen Estrela's tendrils of light. The vine accepted their souls, glowing bright and shaking the earth in response, for I knew that the *Videira* was the single safe place to hide such power and contain what could be used as a weapon against all species.

I blinked several times, coming to and realizing my arms were still outstretched in midair as if the vine were still there in the center of the quiet garden.

Shock echoed throughout my body as I stumbled backward, falling to the uneven ground.

This was a past life I was remembering. I quickly scrambled to my feet, my heart racing inside my chest, before I gripped the edge of the bench as I composed myself.

Bits and pieces of information, of memories, flooded my thoughts. Though blurry, I saw beings flash before my eyes that I once knew, that I once loved dearly. A thousand different emotions tugged at my chest as I heard a man's voice call out my name from the distant past. I could hear the love that resonated within each syllable, his joy that met me from a few feet away, even in his blurry figure.

I was the legendary elf Alizeh in a previous life, one of the first to bloom from the Videira. And I knew where the soul shield was hidden.

The visions, the flashbacks–everything now made sense: why the vine had reacted to mine and Ornella's touch on the day of our ceremony. It wasn't just the vine; it was the souls of my friends from a previous life calling out for help.

I knew what must be done, and now I had an entirely new purpose for my journey back to the five kingdoms: to retrieve the *Saudade* for those who deserved to be whole again.

Bursting with a newfound energy, I sprinted through the maze of paths in the garden, my feet kicking up dirt and rocks. Ornella would be wherever Enid was; she would most likely be preparing for the send-off of the first troops to check the border and see if there were any weaknesses in *Estrella's* defense.

I felt hope rising inside of me, clinging to my resolve. With this pivotal information, my twin might be willing to forgive past transgressions.

I must tell Ornella who I was in a previous life, and who she was to me.

I remembered everything.

If only I had known how vital this moment in time would be, perhaps I would have stopped to smell the flowers and kept the facts to myself. In the back of my mind, I ignored the blaring warning sending butterflies throughout my chest, and instead took it as a sign that I was eager to reveal revolutionary knowledge to Ornella.

If only I had known. Maybe things would have turned out differently.

Chapter Thirty-Six
Lady Gwyneth

The gentle breeze did nothing to cool my flushed skin as I observed the men and women preparing for war on the terrace below. The sun reflected off their armor, and in their optimism, I found only a harsh reminder of the failed attempts at peace. War did nothing but separate us further; the growing void between both realms was a palpable consequence of how greed can forever stain our existence. *There was no way to rewind time; mistakes made cannot be undone.* I gripped the railing on the balcony, tears staining my cheeks. Sayah had entered the area moments before; the look of determination etched across her features.

How many times must I watch this scene unfold?

The two same souls are destined to intertwine, destined to fail. And in each life relived, I watched helplessly as they destroyed one another by choosing what they viewed as righteous. For nothing can be done to stop someone who believes the choices they are making are virtuous, even when the path they are setting ablaze burns what is left of existence in the wake of their narrow-mindedness.

A shadow was cast over my figure as its familiar shape consumed the light encompassing me. For the first time in several thousand lunations, I felt *fear*.

"You knew, didn't you?" he whispered from behind, the blade of his dagger caressing my throat. "You knew that I would be the end of you, and yet you still loved me?"

The shame that coursed through me was unavoidable, and my lip quivered at the touch of his breath on my ear.

"Yes, and I would not change my fate. Because even in knowing that you are my end, all of the moments where you loved me made my life worth living."

I had been gifted the power of sight. What I failed to tell the twins was the extent of my visions and how much of it was fact. I grimaced, my eyes flickering to the girls as they conversed while I awaited death's blow.

How cruel of the Creator to give me such a painful existence, when I had to watch those I loved dearly be reborn and forget who I was, as I witnessed the weight of time gradually corrupt the hearts of those around me.

This is why death is such a vital part of life; without it, souls are left without new beginnings. They are forced to drown in their past sins, which in turn alters their perception of reality.

"I did love you, most ardently," he murmured as he pressed the blade deep into my skin, slicing my neck in one quick movement.

I fell to the marbled stone of the balcony, choking on the blood spilling out of me in a thick river of waves. My hands fluttered to my gaping wound as my body fought for survival when my mind knew it was useless. But I still gazed up at him from the shock of betrayal, my eyes bulging out of their sockets.

He snickered, kneeling in the pool of crimson that surrounded us both. "Gwyneth, it wasn't the visions that killed you. It was the fact that you believed in the potential of what I could be, even when I held the dagger to your throat. You never saw me for who I was; you tried to force your fake illusions and endless possibilities onto my destiny—onto what I wanted."

His truth seeped into my soul as the vibrancy of life withered before my eyes.

Was this what the Creator wanted me to see, all this time? That I was in control of my fate, and my obsession with the future was the cause of my untimely death? How cruel, to learn my most important life lesson in my final moments.

The iron in my mouth was bitter; everything was dark.

A rage shook within me, a hatred for life itself, and it gave birth in my heart as I lay crumpled on the hard ground, gasping for air.

My *Gavinhas* waned, their light dimming as I fought to stay conscious.

"This is the end of who you were and your chance at a new beginning, my darling. I know you want the ability to be in control of your fate, without the limitations set by your gift." Above my face dangled a vile of black liquid, the contents moving of its own volition inside the glass. "And I can give that to you."

In one swift movement, I ripped the vile from his fingers and tipped my head to the sky as I choked and nearly vomited the *Breeder's* blood. I then rolled over onto my back, my chest heaving as it was on the verge of collapsing. The blasphemous magic tightened its grip on my core, slowly suffocating my soul.

It wasn't until after I had taken the poison that I realized the repercussions of my actions. I lay on the stone floor, facing the sky. Tears blotted my eyes, obscuring the white, billowy clouds as they floated by peacefully. It was unjust how life but a few feet away carried on, unaware of my misery. I clenched my jaw and ground my teeth as I simmered in hatred, as the blood dried to my chapped lips. The man whom I loved had tricked me once again in my state of desperation, and this time, he took the most precious thing to me: my ability to reincarnate.

Chapter Thirty-Seven

The creases in our callused hands contain our life's sins,
Brought forth by the actions our hearts are too afraid to face from within,
As weathered storms shake one's constitution,
The evanescent light from the moon sparks joy in the darkest of moments,
Even as our gaping wounds bleed,
Never fully healing,
We choose to love regardless,
We choose to fight—
Despite the unknown;

the uncertainty of uncharted waters,
Our souls found ways to cope as we hide in the shadows,
And triumph still lingers.

THE END

Dear children of the vine,

This letter is for you. Thank you, from the bottom of my heart, for giving my book a chance. There is nothing more enchanting than hearing that someone has read your story. You may have enjoyed it; maybe not. We all have different opinions on art styles, including writing styles and genres. But the fact that you picked up my book to try is truly meaningful to me. This is a letter to those who have helped make my dreams a reality.

And that is highly inspiring—magical, even.

Yours truly,

Victoria M. Sorenson

Author's Bio

Victoria M. Sorenson is the USA's best-smelling author; she exudes the blended fragrance of melancholy tones and a hint of rich sarcasm, paired beautifully with individual notes of floral.

Website:

www.authorvictoriamsorenson.com

Find her on Instagram & TikTok

@victoriamsorenson

Acknowledgements

Hello there, dearest reader.

There is someone special, someone in particular, whom I must share with you, as they have touched my heart deeply, and I need to bring them to your attention. Along my journey, I met a young man named Ajax. It was at a book convention in March 2025, and my interaction with him still lingers with me to this day. You see, I had it in my mind that only young women could enjoy reading my book because of the sweet romance. But Ajax came sprinting up to my table, his eyes wide with a childlike wonder and a massive grin plastered across his face. I immediately began to doubt that he would like my series, but the more I tested the waters with the tropes and the plot, the more he began to jump up and down with excitement. I made him aware of the romance in my book and how it might seem cheesy to him. In that moment, I was direct and asked him if he liked books similar to mine. He simply said, *"Of course!"* Experiencing his reaction planted a seed of inspiration in my soul, one that I have been cultivating and nurturing since.

Also, to Ajax's mom, you are a magnificent mother and deserve to be told this every day.

Abbey, you are one of my favorite human beans, and I'm absolutely going to travel to Canada to meet you in person one of these days. And tell Jonan and the girls I said hello, and that it's time for another trip to the donut shop. You can never have too many sweet treats.

Thank you to my friends, family, and marvelous arc readers. Your support means the absolute realms to me because without you, I am the definition of unorganized chaos. I appreciate you sifting through my box of unhinged comments and overflowing emotions to help me turn this into organized lawlessness. I value you for this and your unwavering, yet gentle encouragement.

And readers, your interactions with authors matter. What you say and how you respond, we remember. We remember your kindness and appreciate your value. So, if you ever get the urge to message your favorite author to tell them how much you loved their book, I implore you to take action. You may not have the ability to see their face light up behind the screen, but I can promise you that we are grinning ear to ear and soaking in your message.